themes of social justice and poverty. *A Christmas Carol in Maine* is explicit in demonstrating the relationship of the privileged class in our country who has failed to address the social issues facing our society. Philip Harris has clearly and unequivocally produced a rich allegory that redefines the importance of Christmas to a new generation of readers.

~Shannon Evans

I0668330

PRAISE FOR A CHRISTMAS CAROL IN MAINE

A Christmas Carol in Maine is a moving replay of the Christmas classic. It comes to life in its portrayal of the character of TJ, a realistic portrait of a disenfranchised youth. He struggles to deal with the loss of his father and fears loving his family in case he loses them also. By becoming totally self-absorbed he only has to think about himself, by putting down others he maintains his wall of uncaring. The author, Philip Harris, has managed to create a sympathetic, understandable character even as TJ scares the elderly and young children alike.

A strong, thorough and meaningful plot is enveloped within of these pages. At around 100 pages, it is a poignant and timely reminder of the meaning of caring in today's world. Its well-chosen words enable a full-length novel to inhabit the pages of a novella. In the guise of the well-loved tale, it reminds us of the effects of modern life, its drugs, wars and poverty, on its people. It gives us the hope and optimism that is much needed in our contemporary world.

This will be a holiday treat for Maine and the country. Put up the holiday lights of all nations, light the fireplace and curl up with this dose of hope.

~Barb Radmore, Editor, Front Street Reviews

I will be completely surprised if we do not see *A Christmas Carol in Maine* as a Hallmark Hall of Fame movie, it is the kind of story families will gladly gather together to enjoy for generations to come."

~Joyce A. Anthony, author of *Storm*.

Not a word is wasted, and you are drawn into the story fairly quickly. The end of the book is a message of hope and it leaves you with a warm feeling that makes you want to hunt out the Christmas tree and curl up with a mug of hot chocolate, even if I did read it in October. A great read.

~Annette Gisby, UK, author of *Silent Screams* And *Shadows of the Rose*

The classic unfolding of the life of a beleaguered and very ill spirited young man faced with the consequences of his own self-serving actions is cleverly layered with messages aimed at the socially irresponsible of our own life and times. *A Christmas Carol in Maine* is a powerful parable of the ills of progressive society left to exist unchecked and held unaccountable. Through the eyes of the spirit guides, Thomas sees that while he is not responsible for the happiness of others, his actions do deeply impact all those who come in contact with him. From the local shop owners to his eight-year-old sister, his exploits leave a deep and lasting impression. Even more critical to note is the tsunami-like wave affect his acts, deeds, and lack of achievement has on those he will never meet. What he does not do with his life is just as significant as what he has done so far in his 16 years.

In Harris' *A Christmas Carol in Maine*, a new family tradition is born. The easy conversational writing style, the logical flow of the story, and the twist to the original story makes this book a new classic that will go on the shelves right next to Dickens' original morality tale. Harris does a marvelous job of weaving Thomas' profound experience of redemption with the underlying

A Christmas Carol
in Maine

Philip F. Harris

ALL THINGS THAT MATTER PRESS

ISBN 13: 9780999524305

Library of Congress Control Number: 2017959238

Second edition.
First edition published in 2006 by Cambridge Books

Illustrations on pages 10, 34, 64, 123 by D.M. Denton
Tree photo by Lionello DelPiccolo

Cover design © by All Things That Matter Press
Published in 2017 by All Things That Matter Press

Dedication

To Deb, As Always, For Always!

For Irene McCollett, who brought Deb into the world, and for Jean Cicienski Harris, who brought *me* into the world.

And for Chantelle, the teenage girl who gave me insights into teen suicide.

Acknowledgments

Charles Dickens published *A Christmas Carol* in 1843. In one manner, shape, or form, this tale has survived and thrived in the hearts and minds of all. Who has not heard the name Scrooge and, at least in jest, muttered the words, "Bah, Humbug?" It is a story of the striving of the human spirit to find meaning in a troubled world. While the times have certainly changed since 1843, there is no question that the world is still troubled.

We often look in all the wrong places in our quest for happiness. Scrooge thought the possession of material wealth would buy peace of mind and "the good life." Instead, it created a hollow shell devoid of friendship, love, and meaning. It was not until he faced his personal "dark night of the soul" that he discovered the need for all of humanity to create a new reality filled with giving, not getting; receiving, not taking. Clearly, a still-timely message for our plugged-in youth who are struggling to find their identity and meaning in a world that plays out in both fantasy and reality on a screen.

Imitation is said to be the highest form of flattery. In some small way, I hope I have been able to imitate the feelings and sentiments that Charles Dickens was able to evoke for so many generations who have sought a higher meaning and purpose of life.

A very heartfelt special acknowledgment to Diane Denton for her wonderful full-size depictions of scenes in the book. She is a wonderful author, artist, and friend.

In addition, to all who have reviewed and commented upon my previous and this revised version of the classic, thank you.

Philip F. Harris

Foreword

Much can be found concerning Charles Dickens and his life. The following are bits of trivia that might not be common knowledge.

Charley Dickens said, "My father was always at his best at Christmas." Charles Dickens loved to celebrate the holiday and his favorite time was Twelfth Night, the feast of the Epiphany.

Early in 1843, in response to a government report on the abuse of child laborers in mines and factories, Dickens vowed he would strike a "sledge-hammer blow ... on behalf of the Poor Man's Child." That sledge-hammer was A Christmas Carol.

It only took Dickens about six weeks to write *A Christmas Carol*. As Dickens wrote *A Christmas Carol* he said that the Cratchits were "ever tugging at his coat sleeve, as if impatient for him to get back to his desk and continue the story of their lives".

"Old Marley was as dead as a door-nail." This line appears toward the beginning of the novel. Dickens included this because of a dream. He had dreamt that one of his good friends was pronounced to be "as dead Sir ... as a door-nail".

The Cratchit family was based on Dickens' childhood. He lived in poor conditions in a "two up two down" four-room house which he shared with his parents and five siblings. Like Peter Cratchit, Charles was often sent to pawn the family's goods when money was tight. Like many poor families, the Cratchits relied on the ovens of their local baker which were available on Sundays and Christmas when the bakery was closed.

A Christmas Carol was first published in 1843 and only six thousand copies of the book were initially printed. The first printing was sold in only five days.

One literary critic called *A Christmas Carol* a "national institution." Dickens' friend, William Makepeace Thackeray, was quick to correct the critic and call the book a "national benefit."

When Dickens wrote *A Christmas Carol*, Christmas wasn't commonly celebrated as a festive holiday. In *The Pickwick Papers* and *A Christmas Carol*, Dickens' descriptions of feasting, games, and family unity helped revive popular interest in many Christmas traditions still in practice today.

In 1867, Dickens read *A Christmas Carol* at a public gathering in Chicago. One of the audience members, Mr. Fairbanks, was a scale manufacturer. Mr. Fairbanks was moved by the reading and he decided to "break the custom we have hitherto observed of opening the works on Christmas Day." Not only did he close the factory on Christmas Day, but also, he gave Christmas turkeys to all his employees. Find more information about Charles Dickens at:

http://www.charlesdickensinfo.com/christmas-carol/trivia/

CHAPTER ONE

 There was one certainty in TJ's life: his father was dead. At first, he didn't believe his mother when she broke the news. He didn't believe it when he saw his grandparents in tears. He didn't believe his aunts and uncles when they came over to the house to console him and his mother.

Now he knew it was true. It was before him in black and white in the *Kennebec Journal,* The *Press Herald,* and the *Bangor Daily News.* It had to be true; there it was, in black and white.

The headlines read: Local Hero Gives Life in Iraq. The story went on to say that Brian Johnson, known to his friends as BJ, gave his life to save three Iraqi children at a Baghdad hospital; that Johnson, a resident of Hallowell and a pediatrician, had been a volunteer doctor in Iraq for the past two years; that when a suicide bomber entered the emergency room, BJ had grabbed the would-be killer and dragged him out of the hospital before the terrorist could detonate explosives that were strapped to his chest; that his heroic act saved the lives of three children who were at the hospital being treated by BJ for minor injuries sustained during a recent firefight between insurgents and local Iraqi forces.

It also said that Brian Johnson had been killed when the bomb detonated.

***

TJ hated that people called him by his initials like they had his father. While it might have been cute when he was a baby, not fully equipped with cognitive abilities, at the ripe old age of thirteen he found the acronyms embarrassing. Not that he and his father were together enough to encounter many of those moments when BJ and TJ would be addressed by their initials, he still disliked the nickname and preferred to be called Thomas. The problem was that no one would listen to him, and the cute childhood name stuck.

Even his baby sister Tara wouldn't succumb to his threats of a thrashing if she didn't call him Thomas. Although she was only five years old, she had a defiant streak that TJ could not penetrate. TJ adored his little sister, with her long straight blonde hair, and deep blue eyes that, in years to come, were destined to make her a heart-breaker. Any time TJ ragged on her to call him Thomas, she'd wrinkle her nose like Shirley Temple, point her finger at him, and say, "I like the name TJ. And I love you, so don't be fussin' with your name." Then she'd smile and hold her arms out for a big hug, and all of TJ's annoyance would melt in his sister's embrace.

His nine-year-old brother Billy was another story. TJ

was Billy's idol, his mentor, his guru, and, in some small way, godlike. Whatever TJ wanted, Billy obliged. Whether it was sharing his toys when he was younger, doing TJ's chores, or rushing out of the bathroom because his brother wanted to use the mirror to comb his hair, Billy did as his brother asked. Billy was also afraid of his brother, who had no problem using threats and physical contact to get his way. TJ had a habit of punching Billy in the upper arm—not the common gesture between friends, but rather a show of force to remind his sibling who was stronger and that TJ wouldn't hesitate to use force to get his way. The problem for Billy was that he would do anything for his brother, including suffering his abuse. It didn't matter who was strongest. Billy loved TJ, and in their father's frequent absences he looked to his big brother for advice and guidance. Further, while Billy occasionally slipped and said TJ, out of love—and fear—he tried to remember to call him Thomas.

***

Now, three years after their father's death, TJ's desires took a life-changing turn.

Over the last three years, TJ had sprouted. At sixteen, he was tall, five feet eleven. He wasn't heavy for his height; his one hundred sixty-five pounds were all muscle. He had chiseled, carved-from-granite, features.

His steel gray eyes kept his classmates at bay and inspired terror in those younger than he. He rarely wore a heavy coat in the winter. It was as if he had an intimate relationship with the heartless cold of the December freeze. The blizzard was his friend, the cold rain his ally. The worse the weather, the better TJ's spirits, for he thrived upon the bleak and the dismal. No one ever stopped him in the halls of school for a casual conversation and ample space was given him where he sat at the back of every class. Teachers never called on him, other than calling his name for attendance.

***

It was a bitterly cold Christmas Eve. A nor'easter was blowing in from the Atlantic and the snowfall was heavy. It had been a dismal day, with fog and snow shrouding the sun. Even the on-early streetlights offered little illumination.

When Hall-Dale High School released its students at 12:25, it was nearly full dark. The stream of cars and buses that left the parking lot moved at a snail's pace on slippery and hard to see roads.

Normally, school would be canceled all day in such a storm, but the track of this unusual front had baffled the best of forecasters. What was supposed to head out into the Atlantic took a quick turn, catching the most experienced meteorologists off guard. Vacation had originally been scheduled to begin several days prior, but the unusual number of storms and school closings so early in the season had forced the administration to stay open right up until Christmas Eve day. Parents weren't any happier about it than their children, but the fact that the school year would already be extended four days into early summer suppressed too many overt complaints.

TJ lived just under three miles from school. Billy always took the bus home. TJ walked, but he waited for the bus to ensure that Billy was on it. With the middle school attached to the high school, it was a short jog for TJ to hook up with his brother. Much to the relief of his fellow students, TJ never rode the bus, regardless of the weather. Today was a little different. While waiting for the arrival of the buses and amid the swirling tendrils snow, TJ heard a voice yell, "Billy, TJ, over here." Uncle Donny was standing on the corner of the small parking lot, his black Envoy fading in and out of view between squalls. Billy grabbed TJ's arm and pulled him over to their uncle's SUV. "Come on, Thomas," urged Billy. "You can't walk home in this." TJ let Billy drag him, slipping and sliding, to Uncle Donny's car. He did *not* intend to get a ride home, but he figured he'd get his brother loaded into the car and then make the cold journey on his own and in his own time.

As the two boys opened the Envoy's door, Uncle Donny shouted in a jovial tone that grated on TJ's bones,

"Merry Christmas, kids."

"Christmas sucks," TJ snarled.

"You don't mean that, TJ."

"I do," TJ said. "And why are you so up on Christmas? It's not like you have lots of money to blow on presents. You barely make over minimum wage. Did you win the lottery or something?"

"Christmas isn't about money and presents. Your aunt and I do just fine, and we count our blessings for all that we have. Why are *you* so down on Christmas? You haven't lacked for anything. I know the loss of your father was a blow, but you were left well taken care of."

TJ repeated, "Christmas sucks."

Billy had jumped into the back seat, but his head hung low.

"Merry Christmas, Billy," Uncle Donny said as he turned to the back seat, a wide grin splitting his face.

In response to the smile, Billy's spirits lifted, and he responded cheerfully, "Merry Christmas to you." A dirty look from his brother dampened his enthusiasm. Once again, Billy hung his head.

"Most people at Christmas just rack up credit bills and go deeper in debt?" TJ said. "It just brings you another step toward bankruptcy. A year older and nothing more to show for your hard work. If I had my way, anyone saying Merry Christmas would be shot … or sent to Iraq."

"TJ," pleaded Donny in a sorrowful voice.

"You do what you want at Christmas and I'll do what I want," TJ said.

"But you don't do anything at Christmas except get depressed and—"

"Just leave me alone," TJ demanded.

"Listen, aside from having fun giving presents and being with the ones you love, there's something joyful about Christmas. It's heart-warming to help others in need. It's fun to share a meal with a friend, sing a few songs, and enjoy the lights and the tree. And although Christmas has never put an extra dollar in my wallet, it does me good to share whatever I do have with others and be thankful for family and friends. I've always felt that way and always will.

"I want you, your mother, Billy, and Tara to come have supper with us tomorrow. Your mother already agreed. It won't be much, but we'll have fun being together as a family," Uncle Donny said.

"I want no part of family and I'll find something of my own to eat. I'm sure Burger King will be open. They make those poor asses work every holiday. The almighty dollar, you know. As for my mother and the rest, they can do what they want. All I want is to be left alone."

With that, TJ slammed the door of the Envoy and faded into the blackness and the cold.

Don shook his head. In the back seat, Billy's eyes swelled with tears. In the tumult of snow and wind, they heard the words "Christmas sucks."

***

TJ veered from the school driveway toward his daily shortcut through the tall pines that ringed the school. He was glad it was Friday. This was the day he met Rudy. Rudy waited by his favorite pine, one obscured from the school and the main road, Maple Street. On this day, they could have met in the parking lot. The darkness, fog, and snow would have provided ample cover. But Rudy preferred the woods. TJ didn't know Rudy's last name and didn't care what it was. All he cared about was that every week Rudy delivered his bag of dope and his joint-to-go. Because TJ was such a good customer, Rudy always had a ready-made joint to send his favorite buyer on his way home.

When TJ reached the tree, he and Rudy did a fist-to-fist tap. "Hey, dude," Rudy said. "Merry fuckin' Christmas."

"Christmas sucks," TJ replied.

"Not after you take a hit of this," Rudy assured him.

TJ pulled the joint out of the bag and used his favorite Zippo lighter to start mellowing out. After a long inhale and a quick cough, he said, "This is good shit, but Christmas still sucks."

"Maybe for you, but this has been a banner year for me. I'm buying my girl a diamond. Cash, dude. I've got money up the ass," Rudy said as he pulled the collar of his coat up around his ears to stave off some of the cold and blowing snow.

"Marriage?" TJ asked.

"Shit, no," Rudy replied. "But she'll will do just about anything if I give her a diamond ... if you get my drift."

"I hear ya."

"Okay, man. I've got to make a few more scores, so I'll catch you next week. Where do you want to meet with school closed and all?"

"At the boat landing," TJ said.

"Cool, dude," Rudy said as he started toward the road. "Merry ... oh yeah, I forgot, Christmas sucks," Rudy said and laughed as he disappeared into the woods.

"Later, Rudy. Hope you get what you want from your girl," TJ shouted. He took another hit and heard a fading voice in the darkness. "You can count on that, man."

TJ stuffed the bag into his hoodie and took yet another hit. As he turned to follow the path out to the road, he was startled by what he thought was a person by the adjacent stand of trees. The image faded with the next gust of wind. *This really is good shit.*

TJ never wore a coat. The black hoodie was his constant companion, no matter the weather. Pulling the hood up over his head, he shoved his hands into his pockets and began his trek downtown, the joint hanging from his mouth. Every few minutes, he'd suck in a lungful of pungent smoke.

Not too many kids were walking home today because many of the parents were off from work early and came to pick them up. He heard the occasional "Merry Christmas" as a few his schoolmates parted company and went their separate ways. Every now and then a car window would roll down and the refrain repeated. In his head, he mimicked the well-wishers. Finally, he yelled at the top of his lungs,

"Christmas sucks." He giggled and repeated over and over in his head, Christmas sucks.

TJ went down Maple Street, made a turn on Greeneville Street, and then took his final left on the main drag to downtown Hallowell. There was almost no traffic; most people had scurried home to their loved ones to begin their holiday celebrations—and to get out of the storm that showed no sign of letting up. He was flying high as the drug took effect and numbed his senses. To his dismay, as he approached downtown, the level of human activity increased. Last-minute shoppers braved the storm to pick up gifts.

TJ had the munchies. That was one of the things he liked most about pot: food tasted so good. He stopped and looked around the City of Hallow, a place that could easily be mistaken for a town out of time. The mostly brick-faced colonial buildings and windows decorated with white electric candles were reminiscent of an eighteenth-century village. The *Antique Capital of Maine* was lined with stores that sported Early American gifts and sundries. Antique offerings could have been the latest in fashion in an earlier age that had no high-tech gadgets and digital items that would end up in overburdened landfills. The old-fashioned street lamps adding to the colonial ambiance were lost on TJ. He was hungry.

He smelled the aroma of Chinese food from the Lucky Garden. His mouth watered for some chicken fingers. Too crowded, he thought. The parking lot was full, and he had no desire to be in the presence of Christmas fanatics and their stupid parties. He stopped suddenly in front of a store called LUX. In the window was a brass horse carousel. He remembered that his mother had commented several times that she wanted that carousel. He'd had no idea what she was talking about, but always asked why she didn't just buy it. Lisa's stock answer was "Some things are meant to be gifts, TJ." Not knowing what she meant, TJ's response was also standard: "Whatever." But for some reason, the carousel drew his attention. Maybe he should get it for his mother for Christmas. TJ shook his head in disbelief that such a thought would even cross his mind and mumbled, "Yeah, right."

He continued down the un-shoveled, slippery sidewalk. Finally, his hunger-heightened sense of smell caught the aroma of baked goods. He started for Slate's Bakery, but movement out of the corner of his right eye caught his attention. There was a large opening between buildings on the east side of the street. Ignoring the slow-moving oncoming traffic, TJ skidded to the rift, which was perhaps once the home of a now-demolished and erased building. Barely able to see the frozen, dark Kennebec River, TJ felt a chill that went to his core. Dancing upon the frozen waters were at least a dozen snow devils, whirlwinds that looked like mini-tornados made of white downy feathers. He was enthralled by their seemingly random, yet orchestrated, ballet as they rose and fell to the beat of the driving winds. However, it wasn't the dancing snow that gave him the chills. Snow devils weren't uncommon. What shook him was the whispered refrain from the fleeting apparitions— Thomaaasss—repeated three times before a gust blew them into the storm.

TJ shook his head to clear his mind. His right hand felt for his stash and once again he thought, "This is really good shit."

The scent of baked goods restored his composure. To the horror of a woman driving her children to their grandparents for a Christmas Eve dinner, TJ stepped into the road without even a glance in either direction. The woman braked too hard and her car began to slide sideways down Water Street. Other vehicles began to pull right or left to avoid collision. If traffic hadn't been already crawling to avoid any potential hazard, downtown Hallowell would have been the scene of a multi-car disaster. The winds and closed windows muffled the screams of the children. TJ smiled at the terrified woman as the car finally came to a stop. She rolled down her window and began to shout. Without looking at her, TJ shouted, "Merry fuckin' Christmas," and then whipped her the finger. He could still hear her yelling as she slowly drove away, tires spinning in search of purchase in the slush.

When he entered the bakery, he pushed his way to the front of the line. No one protested his intrusion. The smell of dope hung heavy on his snow-dampened clothes. Perhaps the few other customers thought the sooner he got what he wanted, the sooner he'd be gone.

He bought several bags of cookies, brownies, and pastries. He had no idea what they were called, but the colors appealed to him. The shoppers were silent as he parted the crowd and returned to the comfort of the storm.

As he left the bakery, he nearly knocked down an elderly woman who was ringing a bell to solicit last-minute donations into her red bucket. TJ looked at her defiantly. Regaining her balance, she said, "Young man, would you care to make a donation to help the needy this Christmas?"

TJ laughed and said, "No, I don't *care*. Did they close the food pantries or something?"

The old woman replied, "Of course not."

"Did they stop giving companies tax breaks for donating to charities?"

"No, they didn't."

"What about the welfare programs? Did they eliminate the Department of Social Services or somethin'?"

"Young man, I am not sure what you mean by these questions, but the need far outweighs the money available," she said.

"Haven't you heard that there are far too many people in the world? Maybe if we didn't try to feed everyone, we wouldn't have so many friggin' problems." TJ got in the woman's face and she backed away a few steps. Much to her relief, the boy spun on his heels and walked away, laughing.

TJ slipped into an alley and rolled another joint. After a few hits, he began to attack his bags of goodies with the fervor of one deprived of food for far too long. Just as he was about to take a bite of a brownie, a snowball slammed the side of his head, causing him to drop his treat. Furious, he turned in the direction of the attack and saw several little kids, his brother included, in the midst of a snowball fight. All of them recognized TJ, froze for a moment, and then scattered like little birds chased by a cat. Only his brother, who, after being dropped off at home, had gone downtown to meet up with his friends, stood still, snowball in hand. TJ beckoned with one finger. Slowly, Billy obeyed. Covered in snow, Billy started to apologize, but TJ halted him with a punch on the shoulder, grabbed another brownie, and continued up the street, leaving his brother in pain but relieved that the punishment wasn't worse.

Billy, rubbing his shoulder, called out, "Hey, guys, it's okay," and ran to rejoin them.

TJ decided to take the long way home, down Water Street, up Winthrop Street, and then back onto Middle Street—more time to smoke and to munch. He also enjoyed watching cars skid up Winthrop Hill for a short while, but that activity soon lost its fascination; there were too many motorists cheerfully helping each other.

He made his final right on Union Street and approached his house.

The large white federal-style home was surrounded by a six-foot iron fence. Built at the end of the 1700s, it was well kept, boasting the charm and grandeur of its earliest days. TJ knew the house would be vacant. Tara was at the sitter's, Billy was out with his friends, and his mother was still probably at work at the D.S.S. She didn't need to work and certainly didn't need the income. Uncle Donny was right, TJ's father *had* left them well off.

TJ's mother was a social worker and sought to fill her days during her husband's long absences by throwing herself into her caseload. Lisa was not the best of mothers. She loved her children, but was terrified of the responsibility of guiding them to adulthood. She bought them anything they wanted, but she couldn't buy what they most needed: her presence. She didn't know how to express her love for them. In her own childhood, she'd never felt the tenderness of a loving parent and so had no frame of reference. In the early days of her marriage, BJ'd taken charge of the kids and played the major parental role. But when his fixation on saving the world kept him away for longer and longer periods, Lisa was not emotionally capable of filling the void. She gave her children lavish allowances, and they always had the latest fads and fashions. And while she could lose herself in the problems of other underprivileged children for eight or ten or twelve hours a day, the fact that they were not hers and she could leave their problems at work made her an effective case worker, but not an effective parent. For Lisa, *do as I say* was much easier than doing for her own.

***

As TJ grew older, he often confronted his mother about this hypocrisy. He would accuse her of helping the "scum of the earth," as he called the less fortunate, but ignoring her own family. To end the arguments, Lisa would usually just throw some money at TJ, which was how he was able to support his habits.

That TJ couldn't get through to his mother depressed and angered him. At least when he was stoned, he could forget about how screwed up his life was for a while.

White electric candles burned in each of the many windows of the house. After unlatching the iron gate, he sloshed his way up the stone walkway. The front door was large and red and trimmed on both sides with black shutters, as were all the windows. On the door was an old-fashioned knocker with the face of a lion. As TJ reached for the handle, he saw the knocker undergo a change and he jerked his arm back. No longer the face of a lion, it had morphed into the face of his father. The face had a dim aura around it, and his father's hair was blowing in the howling wind. His expression was neither angry nor sad, but was one of fatherly concern, a look that TJ remembered from his early childhood—a time he longed to regain. His hair stood up on the nape of his neck and he froze, uncertain as to what to do next.

But as quickly as the image appeared, it disappeared.

TJ hesitantly put his hand on the door handle, drawing back several times to be certain the knocker was staying a knocker, then finally turned the knob and went inside. When he was halfway through the door, he paused and took one more look. Still the face of a lion. He released the breath he hadn't realized he was holding, closed the door, and surveyed the hallway and immediately adjacent rooms. No more specters appeared, and his fear dissipated.

Really weird shit. The weed must be laced with something.

CHAPTER TWO

For the first time in his life, TJ heard the ticking.

After he closed the front door, the only light in the house came from the white candles in the windows and the lighted Christmas tree in the family room to the right of the entrance. To his left was the dining room. Straight ahead was the stair to the bedrooms above. Guarding the entry to the family room was a six-foot-tall grandfather clock. It had stood sentry in that spot since before his birth, a permanent fixture that had never attracted his attention.

What he heard wasn't really a tick, but more like the sound of a horse's hoof on cobblestone, repeating in time with the clock's pendulum. TJ stopped to look at the clock, but saw nothing unusual. As he turned to go up the stairs to his room, the sound became louder. He paused on the first step and turned to study the clock a second time. The sound grew louder, each beat vibrating into the next. TJ put his hands to his ears to try to muffle the deafening crescendo. The noise grew until he fell to the floor and wrapped his arms over his head in an attempt to end the assault on his senses. Suddenly, there was silence. He stayed on the floor for a moment, uncertain it was over, then stood, eyes fixed on the clock.

He could barely hear it.

"TJ, is that you?" The sound of a voice made TJ jump.

"Jesus Christ, Lisa! You scared the shit out of me," TJ said.

"Watch your mouth, young man," Lisa said.

"Well, it's not polite to sneak up on people," TJ said.

"How is it sneaking to pull in the driveway and come in the way I always do?"

"Well, you should learn to make more noise."

His mother shook her head. She'd given up trying to figure out her oldest son—and she hated that he called her Lisa. That had started just before BJ left on his last trip to Iraq, just before his death. She didn't understand why she'd gone from Mom to Lisa, but her protests were useless. On Christmas day three years ago, TJ changed. No matter how hard she tried, there'd been no stopping her son's transformation.

"What are you doing home so early anyway? Where's Tara?"

"Your uncle picked her up, grabbed Billy from downtown, and took them to his house. The storm's bad and we decided to spend the night there in case we all get snowed in. You saw him after school, right? He told you we're all going to have Christmas dinner there? " She tried to keep her tone pleasant.

"Yeah, I saw him, and I told him I wasn't going. I'm sure he told you that, too."

Ignoring his response, she said, "With the weather so

bad we decided it would make more sense to have our tree tomorrow afternoon. I'm going to bring over a few of the gifts so Billy and Tara will have a good morning and then after dinner we'll come back and kind of have a second Christmas with the gifts I leave here."

"Do whatever you want. I'm not going," TJ said. "Christmas sucks anyway."

"Damn it, TJ, do you always have to try to ruin everything? You know Billy and Tara will be heartbroken if you don't come. Can't you think of someone but yourself for a change? Would it really kill you to show a little holiday spirit? Besides, I don't want to leave you here alone in this storm. We may lose power. You know how CMP is this time of year. The power goes out all the time."

"Since when are you so concerned about leaving me alone? You're always running around trying to help your trailer trash bums and welfare brats. We're always left alone, so why should today be any different?"

A tear rolled down Lisa's cheek. Every time she tried to talk to TJ, they fought. Yes, she often worked long hours, but, in her mind, the kids were always cared for. She wondered why he couldn't he understand that people don't choose a life of poverty, that they're trapped in it, and don't know how to get out. She wiped the tear with her blouse sleeve and refused to continue the argument. There were two others, though not yet of an age that required a lot of attention on her part, that she hadn't lost, and she wasn't going to spoil their Christmas. She took a deep breath.   "Fine. I'm going to grab a few things and head over to your uncle's. If you change your mind, call a taxi. I'll leave some money on the counter." She pulled a twenty-dollar bill out of her wallet and laid it down in front of her son before stuffing some presents into a bag.

Once she was ready to leave, Lisa added in a last attempt to make peace, "Sure you won't change your mind?"

"I'm sure," he said. "Thanks for the contribution."

Lisa knew how her son spent his money but didn't know how to deal with it. It was easy to give a speech to her clients because she knew she could then walk away. Ultimately, they were not her direct responsibility. But any attempt to dissuade TJ fell on deaf ears. She somehow couldn't find the right words to say.

"Fine," she said. "Merry Christmas." She grabbed her bags and purse and went out the back door. TJ heard his mother scraping off the windshield and then the hum of the car leaving the driveway. He looked at the clock, then glanced around the dimly lit house. He was about unplug the lights on the tree, but hesitated and instead went upstairs to his room.

CHAPTER THREE

 TJ's room was a mother's worst nightmare. It was large, with plenty of closet space, but TJ had no use for hangers—or hampers. Clothes were strewn everywhere. The only hint of a bed was the pile of shirts, jeans, and hoodies that rose higher against one wall. The one neat spot in the room was a corner that boasted a state-of-the-art entertainment center with a CD player at center stage. Picking up a remote control, TJ hit the play button and the silence was broken by an ear-shattering cacophony of beats that shook the posters of the Victoria's Secrets models on his walls. Still a little shaken by the clock incident, TJ looked around the room and went to the unused closet. Finding nothing but more mess and empty hangers, he closed his bedroom door and locked himself in.

As he was pulling off his hoodie he heard a low click, click, click sound from his dresser. It was covered with CDs and X-Box games, but he could still see the kinetic energy device that sat on one corner, its metal balls suspended on strings. When the first ball was moved, it would hit the second. Energy was transferred through four other balls that would remain stationary, but the sixth ball would swing out as if struck directly by the first. The click, click, click sound grew louder as the balls swung faster. He could hear the noise above the blaring music, which suddenly stopped playing. The clicking became deafening, but then, as quickly as it had begun, it stopped.

Rudy must tell me what he put in the weed.

He was about to check his CD player when he felt a draft. He looked around the room and verified that the windows were shut and locked. He could hear a rustling movement outside his door, like a wind blowing in the rest of the house. The sound grew in volume, and he wondered if he had remembered to close the front door. Maybe it blew open.

As he started to leave his room, he sensed pressure building outside his door. The clothes in his room began to move as the draft became a whirlwind. A pair of jeans flew in his face followed by socks and shirts. He sought the protection of his bed and dove under a pile of blankets and comforters. These, too, began to be pulled by the wind. He clung to them. He heard a loud pop explode in the air. The winds suddenly abated.

Silence. Cautiously, he removed the blankets from over his head.

He looked toward the bedroom door and there stood his father. Behind him—or, rather, through him—Thomas saw that his door was still closed. The specter of his father was transparent, but Thomas could see all his features. BJ was tall, six-foot-three. His hair was the color of rust, neat and trim. His build was lean, a trait inherited by his son. BJ was wearing a white medical coat, stained and torn in several places, that fell to the middle of his thighs. Thomas rubbed his eyes, trying to clear the apparition from his sight.

"You don't believe it's me, do you, Thomas?" his father said. Normally, he'd called his son TJ, but he knew his son wanted people to use his proper name.

"No, I don't," TJ said.

"Why don't you believe what your own eyes tell you?"

"One reason is because I'm stoned. Secondly, Rudy probably laced my dope with something. For all I know, I fell asleep and you're a nightmare caused by all the brownies or that other fancy chocolate thing I ate." TJ fell back on the sarcasm he used in tense situations. Sometimes he could scare people bigger and tougher than himself just by knowing what words to use. His mouth got him in trouble, but it often saved his ass. "You see this?" He pulled out his bag of pot.

"I do," his father said.

"If I want to see ghosts or mess up my mind, all I need to do is smoke a lot of this. I can create all the monsters I want with this or a lot of other stuff that's easy to buy."

His father raised a cry that turned TJ's defiance into fright. TJ cowered. To his horror, his father opened his tattered coat and revealed the effects of a terrorist's bomb on the human body. TJ screamed and covered his eyes against the image of shredded organs and missing body parts. He began to sob.

"Why are you doing this to me?"

"Do you believe it's me or not?" his father demanded as he slowly closed his jacket.

"I do, I do," TJ said, still crying. "But why are you here?"

"I didn't do what I should have while alive, so I must do it in death. What I didn't accomplish then I must try to accomplish now if I'm to move to the Light."

TJ raised his eyes to his father's face. "I don't follow you. This is freaking me out."

"I know it's hard to understand. There are things I should've done when I was home that I didn't do. If I can't correct those mistakes, then, when I live again, I'll have to repeat those life experiences. They'll be in a different place and a different time, but the scales must be balanced. If I can correct those mistakes now and prevent you from taking the wrong path, I'll be able to move on."

TJ pondered what his father had said and then asked, "Are you in some kind of hell?"

"In a way, but it's one of my making." BJ looked despondent, almost on the verge of tears.

"I still don't understand. You were always gone, doing things for other people," TJ said. "And what do you mean, when you live again?"

BJ sighed. Pictures on the wall began to shake, and TJ

shrank back in fear. "That is the crux of the matter," his father said. "As you got older, I was always gone, dealing with the needs of others while ignoring those of the ones I loved the most. I had to learn that my own house must be in order if I truly want to help others. My ego and selfish pride kept me from reaching this goal. Oh, yeah, I gave you all the material things. You wanted for nothing except what I refused to give because I had more *important* things to do. I had to go make my mark in the world, not realizing I already had."

The specter moaned again. "Life continues, Thomas, it is never-ending, and we must, each and every one of us, face the consequences of our actions."

TJ was not at all certain he understood his father's words. The only part that really hit home was his father's admission of not being around when he needed him the most. Those words cut deeply into TJ's heart and he filled with a mixture of sadness and anger. BJ's trips to parts unknown to save the world had left the family in an emotional vacuum. His mother didn't fill the void. When she wasn't doing her bit to save others, she moped around the house as if seeking some form of comfort not to be gained from her children. The comfort and support she sought were halfway around the world. Instead of filling the parental gap, she filled their pockets with money or bought them anything they wanted. Billy and Tara were able to cope with their father's absence and their mother's distance, but TJ had needed more.

Perhaps it was their age or perhaps they just didn't know the difference. They grew up with their father's absence and didn't remember a time when Lisa was any different. TJ wasn't sure he did, either, but there was a nagging elusive memory of a time when life was better.

"Hear me, Thomas," his father said. TJ's mind snapped back to his surreal meeting with his dead father. "My time grows short. I don't understand how I'm able to appear to you now. For the past three years, I have sat by your side in sadness and despair."

TJ wondered if that was the reason for the occasional chill that came from nowhere, even on the hottest summer day.

"I'm here to tell you that you may yet escape the horrible world that you are creating. You will be visited by three spirits."

"I think I'd rather pass on that. My world is fine," TJ said with uncertainty.

Ignoring his son's words, BJ pronounced, "The first will come at midnight, the second at one, and the third at three."

"Really, I'm okay. I ... I'm going to be fine. Seeing you has made a big difference. No need for the others, really."

"Without them, yours will be a life of sorrow and despair. "Remember what I've told you, my son, and what has passed between us. I won't be able to come this way again, of that I'm certain."

With these last words, his father's image began to fade. Transparent tears ran down his face. TJ saw his father say, "I love you." A gale materialized from nowhere, and, with another loud pop, his father disappeared, the room was silent. TJ looked around the room and it all looked normal. Everything was just as it had been when he came home.

He was emotionally and physically exhausted and flopped back onto his bed. His last thought before sleep was *Rudy, I am going to kill you the next time we meet.*

CHAPTER FOUR

 It was midnight. The house was silent. TJ began to toss and turn and grope for the covers as a chill filled the room. Frost began to form on the windows. He awoke from his restless sleep and his body was covered with goosebumps. He slowly sat up, wrapping his arms around himself to stay warm. He thought, shit, the power's out. A flashing light caught his attention. His electric alarm clock on the end table beside his bed was flashing 12:00—12:00—12:00. He concluded that the power was on.

He noticed that each breath he took was visible. He shivered, grabbed his comforter, and pulled it around his shoulders. Did the furnace kick off? he wondered. He stood and pulled the comforter even tighter around his body. Glancing around the room, he saw that frost had coated every surface.

His attention turned to the closet door that supported a full-length mirror. A small blue-white light began to form in its center. "What the ...." Still shivering, he looked around in search of the source of what he thought was a reflection. Suddenly, the power went out and both the inside and outside world went terribly dark—except for the growing swirl of light from *within* the mirror.

TJ shielded his eyes and began to move toward it as the cold bluish light grew brighter and increased in size, driving him backward with its intensity. His knees hit the back of the bed and he lost his balance and collapsed. The light escaped from the mirror and coalesced into human form. In total disbelief, TJ watched the light take on the image of his old girlfriend, Chantelle, who had committed suicide the year before.

"Jesus Christ," he exclaimed. "Chantelle, is that you?"

TJ rose from the bed and approached the apparition of his lost love. His comforter fell from his shoulders as he took several tentative steps in her direction.

She backed away a few feet to avoid his touch.

"Don't touch me, Thomas. My stay in this world is brief and physical contact would break the spell."

TJ lowered his hands, fearing the loss of this vision. "Is it really you?"

"It is."

Chantelle was dressed in blue jeans, a white pullover jersey top, and her trademark combat boots. Her auburn hair was still shoulder-length, and her slight build accentuated her figure. Gradually, the cold blue light began to fade to a soft glow that radiated only a few inches from her skin.

"Are you the spirit my father said would come?" TJ asked.

"I'm the first, and time is short. We must go," she said, and her hand pointed toward the mirror.

"Whoa," he said. "Do you think that you can just suddenly appear through a … a … mirror and expect me to follow you? Chantelle, so much was unsaid between us. I … I don't know why you did what you did. Your death was the final blow that threw me over the edge. We had a thing going. I was so close to losing it when my father died, but you were there, at least for a while. Then you left me, too. You cut your damned wrists and left me all alone. Why did you do that? Why did you have to go? I thought you loved me. You did, didn't you? Christ, Chantelle, you left me hanging and … and … what the hell happened?" Tears filled his eyes and his muscles twitched uncontrollably.

"We don't have time, Thomas. We must go," she insisted.

"Well, make time. I'm not going anywhere until I get some answers," he said.

Chantelle looked beyond Thomas and appeared to be having a conversation with an unseen being. She finally nodded her head in agreement. She turned to him and said, "I have been given a few moments. Listen to my story.

"When we met, I was thirteen years old. Before we met, I had lived in Gardiner. Then I moved to Chelsea and attended Hall-Dale and you and I got together. My stepfather was a drug addict. My real dad died in a car accident when I was only two."

TJ sat back on the bed, his eyes glued on Chantelle. Without the slight glow around her body, he would have sworn she was still alive and that they were having one of their late evening chats.

As if reading his mind, Chantelle said, "No, Thomas, I'm dead to this world. I must hurry with this story—you have much to see this night.

"As you well know, I've never looked my age and always passed for older. Unfortunately, my stepfather also thought I was 'well developed.' One night my mother came home early from shopping. My stepfather was drunk, and he had me on his lap. My mother went into a rage. She yanked me off him, picked up a beer bottle, and smashed it over his head. He was able to get to a hospital, but we never saw him again.

"After that night, my mother turned to God. She said we were unclean and had to be saved. She filled the house with pictures of Jesus and every grotesque crucifix she could buy. She threw out all my jeans, makeup, and music. She said they were evil. She kept me from seeing my friends, saying they were a bad influence and needed to be saved before she'd let me talk to them. I had to keep clothes at my girlfriend's house. Mother thought we were studying the Bible together. My friend's name was Paige. She put on a good act for my mother and was always prim and proper and saying 'Praise Jesus' when my mother was around. I started doing drugs. Paige had a seventeen-year-old brother and we partied every chance we got. Jimmy was awesome, at first. After a couple of months, though, he started to get mean. He hit me at some of the parties to show off in front of his friends. I was covered with bruises.

"After being abused by my stepfather and my boyfriend and smothered by my mother, I started to cut myself. I guess I thought I was bad and deserved the pain. Or that it was the only way to let the pain out. Or both.

One night my mother caught me drinking with Paige and Jimmy. She went berserk and beat me almost to death. That was when I was put into foster care at a house in Chelsea.

"At first, everything was fine at the foster home. My foster dad worked second shift and I rarely saw him. My foster mom was cool. I know you never met her, but she didn't mind when we started seeing each other. She wouldn't let boys at the house, but she didn't care what we did as long as we didn't attract the cops. Then, like I told you, my foster dad got laid off from the shipyard. That's when it got to be harder to see you. He began to drink a lot. He wanted me to stay home more often and started to rub up against me. Then one day he came home shitfaced. He pulled me into his bedroom and … and … my step mom just stood in the doorway, watching. She kept saying, 'It's okay, don't say anything, I can't afford to lose the payments.' She must have said that twenty times.

"I lost it, Thomas. That's why I did what I did."

TJ was in tears. He didn't know what to say. He stood, picked up his alarm clock, and threw it across the room. "I'll kill that son-of-a-bitch," he screamed.

Chantelle hung her head for a moment, took a deep breath, and said, "Will you come with me now?"

"Yes."

Chantelle pointed at the mirror. "I'll go first." She

turned and went into it. TJ could still see her, and she beckoned him to follow. Hesitantly, he walked through.

CHAPTER FIVE

Thomas found himself at the entrance to a run-down trailer park. Everything was encased in a surreal halo, including Chantelle. She held out her hand and Thomas said, "I thought I couldn't touch you."

"That was back there," she said, nodding to the still visible mirror. "I'm of this world now and as real as you."

Thomas reached for and held her waiting hand. He was surprised that it was warm to the touch and not cold and dead. He squeezed gently, and they shared a brief smile.

"Why have you brought me here? I've never been in a place like this."

"I'm here to show you the past," Chantelle said.

"I have no past here," Thomas protested with a look of disgust as he surveyed the pallid surroundings.

"There is much you don't know or understand," Chantelle said. Just then, a little boy came running around one of the trailers. He splashed through a puddle, ran straight towards Chantelle, and then ran right through her.

"What the hell?" Thomas said.

A moment later, a small border collie also came down the road and ran not around, but through, his legs. "Holy crap! How did they do that?" he asked as he checked his body to see if it was solid. To his touch, it was.

"These are images of things past. They have no consciousness of our presence." Chantelle replied.

"This is very cool," Thomas said. "But this place has nothing to do with my past."

Chantelle walked away from him and went in the direction from which the boy and pup had come. Thomas followed and then came to an abrupt halt. On the steps of one of the trailers sat a young girl playing with a tattered doll. The girl appeared to be only seven or eight, but Thomas thought she looked familiar. He started to ask who she was, but he then heard a voice call out, "Lisa, get your ass in here and clean this house. And stop playing with that stupid doll. You're too old for that crap and too old to be sitting around doing nothing."

The little girl said, "Yes, Momma. I'm sorry." She tucked the doll under the broken steps and went into the trailer.

"Is that—"

"Yes, that's your mother," Chantelle said.

"Lisa grew up in a dump like this?"

"She did, Thomas."

"I never knew her background. She never talked about her past. She said her parents died when she was young. She never said that she came from a place like this."

"There's a lot you don't know." Chantelle walked

around the trailer and TJ followed. He looked in as he passed. He had no idea his mother had grown up in such squalor.

When Thomas rounded the corner, he pulled up short, like a horse that balks at a jump that's too high. He was on a busy corner in Harvard Square. The only reason he knew this location was that he stood in front of a store that said Harvard Square Coffee Shoppe. It was raining, and people scurried about with umbrellas while trying to avoid splashes from passing cars. Chantelle pointed into the coffee shop. Once again, Thomas saw his mother. She was standing behind the counter in a light blue waitress uniform, pouring a cup of coffee.

"Damn, that's my father," he said. The rain changed to snow. TJ looked around and suddenly noticed the square filled with Christmas lights and bundled-up pedestrians carrying shopping bags filled with bright boxes. He turned to Chantelle.

"Yes, it's Christmas Eve."

Without another word, she moved toward the entrance of the coffee shop. The door opened in anticipation of her passage. Thomas gave one more glance at the Christmas lights glowing in the heavy falling snow and followed Chantelle.

He began to run towards his parents, but Chantelle stopped him. "Remember, they can't see or hear you. This is a place out of time."

Thomas looked at Chantelle and nodded sadly. There was a vacant stool beside his father and Chantelle silently indicated he could take the seat. He sat beside his father and looked back and forth from one parent to the other.

As Lisa poured BJ his coffee, he gently caressed her hand. "BJ, you're going to make me spill this," she said.

"I'll clean it up. It's worth it just to touch you."

"Well, it may be worth it to you, but I can't afford to lose my job because I'm flirting with the customers."

With feigned indignation he said, "And just how many customers do you flirt with?"

"Only you, lately." With a big smile, she turned to wait on another customer.

BJ smiled back and watched her every move. Thomas was almost embarrassed by the way his father was looking at his mother. "Oh waitress, waitress," BJ said. Few of the other customers paid him much mind. They all seemed absorbed in checking shopping lists and finishing their brief snacks before heading back out into the growing snowstorm.

"Waitress," he said again, "A little more coffee, please?" Thomas noticed that his father was so busy watching Lisa that he hadn't even taken a sip of the coffee that he had.

Lisa finally came back to BJ and began to pour without looking at the cup. The black liquid overflowed onto the counter.

"Oh, my God, I'm so sorry," she said.

"Will you marry me?" BJ said.

"What?"

"Will you marry me?" He shouted. All eyes in the shop turned to them.

Lisa turned a blushing red and said, "Yes!"

A round of applause broke out and as Lisa bent over the counter to hug her husband-to-be. Thomas heard the customers saying, "Merry Christmas."

Thomas yelled, "Yes." He tried to hug his father and mother, but his arms passed through their bodies. He gave up in frustration. With a pleading expression, he looked towards Chantelle, but she shook her head. He turned back to his parents as they gradually disappeared into a cloud of dissipating steam. The coffee shop dissolved, and he found himself back on the street in the snow. Chantelle walked away, went around a corner and was out of sight. He followed her. When he turned the same corner, he found himself standing in the warmth of a huge living room. An older woman was sitting in a leather wingback chair, sipping a cup of tea. The room had Queen Anne furniture, too many vases flowers, and too many paintings of flowers. Thomas disliked the décor and was about to comment, but then he saw his father.

"I think you are making a big mistake, Brian," the old woman said. "Why you feel you must marry that trailer trash is beyond my understanding."

"Mother, she is not trash. She's attending a fine university and will soon have her graduate degree. Please don't talk about her that way."

"What good is a degree to poor people?"

"Mother, I will not have you talk that way. She's getting her Masters in social work. Don't be so prejudiced," he said.

"That hardly compares to your degree from Harvard Medical. You should marry according to your station. Her station is the other side of the tracks."

"Enough, mother. We're getting married with or without your blessing."

"You go, Dad," Thomas yelled. They didn't hear him.

***

Once again, the room melted away. He found he was standing in the hallway of a house filled with an aroma of pine and spruce. It was an old refurbished colonial home with white candles in all the windows and a huge fresh balsam fir in the picture window. The eight-foot tree strung with popcorn and cranberries and wrapped in blinking, multi-colored lights was a welcoming sight.

CHAPTER SIX

Thomas could see falling snow through the small panes of the window that had begun to frost in the corners. The glow from the candles added to the atmosphere of a picture book New England Christmas. He could hear laughter and giggling from upstairs, accompanied by the stomping of little feet.

He turned to Chantelle to ask what was happening, but she said, "Shh, you'll see."

He looked again at the tree with its gigantic mound of presents, boxes in all sizes, shapes, and colors, each meticulously wrapped with a matching bow. Then he saw it, tucked in a corner to one side of the tree, partially obscured by the boxes: a bright red tricycle with a siren attached to the handlebar. All three tires were whitewalled and the silver spokes reflected the colors of the Christmas tree lights. "Oh, my God," he whispered.

Suddenly, two little people in pajamas came crashing down the stairs and halted abruptly in the archway to the living room. It was his brother Billy and TJ himself.

Just as the two excited young boys were about to attack the pile of presents, they heard from upstairs, "You know the rules," their father said, "Into the kitchen, both of you."

"Aw, Dad, do we have to?" TJ said.

"Yes, you have to," their mother replied.

Thomas turned to Chantelle and said, "My parents were sadists. Really. On Christmas morning, they'd set our stockings against our bedroom door. Billy and I shared a bedroom until he was around nine years old, so that was a lot of fun. However, here's where the sadism comes in. Rather than let us get up and go to the tree to open presents, they made us have breakfast first,"

"No. You're kidding, right?" Chantelle said.

"Seriously, they were twisted people. They'd get up right behind us, let us see the presents, and make us go into the kitchen so they could have coffee and smoke a half a pack of butts. Then they made us some cereal, or toast, or something, and made us sit there in agonizing anticipation until they were good and ready."

Chantelle laughed. "That is simply horrible. I love it."

"Well, Billy and I didn't think it was a laughing matter." TJ watched as his younger, carefree parents walked hand-in-hand down the stairs and into the kitchen. As they passed, Thomas started to put out his hand to touch his parents, but he remembered the coffee shop and knew it would be futile. He almost laughed as little Billy and TJ followed, their heads constantly turning to look at the tree.

Thomas and Chantelle followed and watched as his father poured the coffee and sat with Lisa for what seemed like an eternity. They had taken only a bite or two from the bowls of Shredded Wheat and Cheerios when, at last, his father stood and said, "Well, are you two going to see what Santa brought or do you want some—"He was unable to complete his question as the two boys sped past their father and into the living room.

Thomas started to follow, but Chantelle held up her hand and said, "Wait."

"But I want to see my ... I mean TJ's face when he finds that bike. I wanted a bike like that so bad. Billy was still too young to get one, and, man, was he jealous when he saw it. At first, I didn't think Santa left one because it was buried behind all the other presents. Then there it was in all its red glory. It was so beautiful and shiny. I thought I was going to die of sheer excitement."

"You were very happy then?"

"Friggin' A, I was," Thomas said.

"Listen to your parents," Chantelle said.

Thomas, still wanting to follow himself into the living room, agreed and turned his attention back to his mother and father. Lisa took BJ's free hand and said, "I want to give you your first present out here."

"Don't you think the kids might pop their heads back in? It would be embarrassing, you know," BJ said with a sly grin.

Lisa gently slapped his hand and said, "Not that kind of present, you big jerk. Besides, you got that one last night."

"I know, but I wouldn't mind another one," BJ said.

"You know I'm not a morning person, especially when it comes to that," Lisa said.

"Okay, then where's my first present?" BJ asked as he looked about the kitchen for a wrapped box.

Lisa stood up and pointed to her stomach. "This is your present," she said with a big grin.

"Lisa, I have a stomach. I don't need another one."

"My God, you're so dense. Not my stomach, what's inside, you moron."

For a brief moment BJ didn't have a clue, then said, "You mean—"

"You betcha," said Lisa. "It's a girl!"

BJ jumped out of his chair, grabbed Lisa, and twirled her around in circles. Both were laughing, and BJ began to sing, "Joy to the world ...." He set Lisa down and told her that the news was the best present he could get. BJ was all into the boys and knew that Lisa's heart was set on a baby girl. "When did you find out?" BJ asked.

"The ultrasound came back yesterday. I was bursting to give you the news."

"Let's go tell the boys," BJ said. He grabbed Lisa's hand and they charged into the living room. Thomas and Chantelle followed. "I remember this," Thomas said.

As they entered the living room, his parents could barely move without tripping over boxes, getting tangled in ribbon, or crunching wrapping paper. Little TJ was plowing a path through the disaster zone with his siren blaring.

Thomas was laughing at the all the confusion.

Not sure what to do, BJ yelled, "You're going to have a baby sister." There was a brief lull.

TJ jumped off his bike, went up to his mother, and then stood silent for a couple of seconds. He then looked his mother square in the eye and both TJ and Thomas said in unison, "Her name is Tara." TJ turned and went back to riding his bike. Billy wasn't sure what was going on, so he kept playing a game on one of his new electronic toys.

Both of his parents, looking at first bewildered, began to laugh until finally Lisa said, 'Then Tara it is."

***

The room, his parents, Billy, TJ, and the entire house began to waver. The image blurred and faded. Thomas said to Chantelle, "Just a little longer, pleeease?"

There was a moment of total darkness. When the light returned, Thomas saw an older TJ on a set of swings in his former backyard. TJ was not swinging, just sitting in the seat. Off to the side he caught a glimpse of Billy and Tara as they ran around the house, yelling and screaming while they squirted each other with their water cannons.

BJ was sitting on the grass beside his oldest son.

CHAPTER SEVEN

"Dad, why do you have to go again?" TJ said in the squeaky voice of a thirteen-year-old. "You've only been home for a few weeks. What about my baseball practice and my games? I never do any good unless you're there."

"Now, son, you know that's not true. You're a great ballplayer. Besides, I should be home around Christmas. And remember, your mother needs all the help she can get, so you have to be the man of the house while I'm gone," BJ said.

"Lisa doesn't—"TJ started to say, but his father cut him off.

"I told you, do not call your mother by her first name."

"Sorry, Dad. Mom doesn't need my help. She just plays with Tara when she's home, which isn't all that much. She may not be in another country like you, but she might as well be. She spends all of her time helping those poor people." TJ kept his head down and wouldn't look his father in the eye.

Calmly, knowing TJ got upset anytime he left, BJ said, "We've covered this ground before, TJ. Those poor people need all the help they can get. You don't know what it's like to be hungry, thirsty, homeless, or sick, and without hope of getting any help. And, while things aren't quite as bad in the good old U.S. of A., there are still a lot of people who need the kind of help your mother gives them."

Defiantly, TJ said, "Then why don't you stay here and help them? I can't even pronounce the names of the places you go to."

"Because, as I've told you in the past, I have skills that are desperately needed in those places that you can't pronounce. They have no doctors, TJ, and the children need medical help. You wouldn't believe the diseases they get. At least here there are plenty of doctors and almost everyone can get some medical help."

"Well, if you were home, Mom would be a lot happier and at least one of you would be around," TJ said.

"Son, I know this is hard for you, but it's not like you're lacking for anything. You have your brother and sister, you live in a beautiful home, and most kids don't have one tenth of the things you do. Maybe soon I won't go away as much, and we'll get to spend more time together."

"You say that every time you leave, but it never happens," TJ said. He jumped off the swing and ran down the street, destination nowhere.

Thomas and Chantelle followed his father as he went into the house. Lisa would soon be taking her husband to the airport, so she'd taken the day off. Thomas was upset; old fears and anger were beginning to surface. Thomas watched his father hug Lisa and then they sat at the kitchen table.

"Did you tell him?" Lisa asked.

"He ran off before I really had a chance to," BJ replied.

"I really worry about him," Lisa said. "I don't know how to handle him anymore. Every time you go, he seems to sink deeper and deeper into himself. He picks on his brother, won't give me the time of day, hides out in his room, and he's starting to call me Lisa."

"I know. It's the *in thing* to call your mother by her first name. I told him not to," BJ said.

"Well, he gets it from that new crowd he's hanging with. He won't even bring them by for me to meet. Says that's little kid stuff. I'm really worried, BJ. Thank God this'll be your last overseas trip. He needs your firm hand at this point in his life. To him, being with his mother is an embarrassment. Early teens are not a good place these days for one parent. I wish you had the chance to tell him that you were re-opening your practice in Augusta." Lisa looked worried and was almost tearful.

BJ got up and put his arms around her. "I'm already scheduled for my return flight on Christmas day. Do me a favor, please don't tell him. I want my return, and my stay, to be his big Christmas present. When he sees I'm back for good, we'll be a tight family again, and I know he'll be fine. Just a relatively few short months and all will be well. You know that I love that guy to death. It'll be just fine," BJ said.

Thomas stood in shock, tears streaming down his face. "Chantelle, why didn't my mother tell me?"

"She promised your father, Thomas," Chantelle said. "There was no reason for her to believe things would *not* be okay when your father returned. There was no reason for her to believe he wouldn't return. He wasn't in the danger zone. Who knew that what happened could happen?"

"Why didn't she tell me when he died?"

"Two reasons. She was too devastated." Chantelle paused.

"And the second?"

"You never gave her the chance," Chantelle said and walked away.

***

Once again, the house and his parents began to dissolve. Thomas felt a breeze, which turned into a wind, and then a whirlwind. He felt he was in the center of a tornado. As quickly as it began, it ceased. Thomas found himself, exhausted, back in his own room. Chantelle was standing beside him.

"Shortly, you will be visited by another spirit, one that may surprise even you. I hope you've learned a few things from my presence. It's the old saying, Thomas, 'if only I'd known then what I know now.' Be at peace, my lost love. Perhaps in another time, in another place."

Chantelle began to melt into the mirror from which she appeared.

"Do you have to go, Chantelle? There's so much I'd like to say and talk about," Thomas said, tears coursing down his cheeks.

"Rest, Thomas. We lose so many opportunities to say what could be said. You still have much to see."

He could barely keep his eyes open as Chantelle and the mirror became one. Then she was gone. Thomas sat on his bed, emotionally drained. Within moments, he was sleeping.

CHAPTER EIGHT

 The air grew heavy in his room. Beads of moisture formed on the windowpanes and zigzagged this way and that as gravity pulled them down to the wooden dividers. Thomas was still asleep, sweat on his brow. He kicked the comforter off his legs and began to toss and turn in a futile effort to find comfort.

Thomas bolted upright. He pinched himself to make sure that he was awake. The pain convinced him. With his shirtsleeve, he wiped the moisture from his forehead. Looking out the window, he saw the storm still in full force. Noticing the rivulets of water on the windows, he couldn't understand how the moisture remained unaffected by the chilled outside air. He thought that maybe the thermostat had kicked up. How he didn't know. He glanced at his alarm clock. It was flashing 1:00—1:00—1:00.

He looked at the mirror. Nothing was happening. He looked around the room, but aside from the heat, there was nothing unusual. Nothing was out of place. Nothing was moving. There were no unusual sounds. He prepared himself for almost anything, yet nothing was happening. Five minutes, then ten, then fifteen went by, but all was still and quiet. Thomas began to doubt that anything at all had occurred. Perhaps the drugs caused his visions. *It was so real. Chantelle's hand, my father's voice, Mom's laughter, the bike ... all the experiences were so real.*

Something caught his eye. Not a movement, but a light. It came from outside the closed door of his bedroom. He knew there were no lights on in the house. He slowly stood and took several tentative steps towards the door. While a few moments earlier he'd been ready for his next visitor, now he wasn't so sure. The notion that his father and Chantelle were illusions from a bad trip faded.

The moment his hand touched the doorknob, a soft voice called his name and told him to enter. For the first time in several years, he did as he was told without question.

He walked into his own room. There was no mistake. It was his room. He turned to look back, but all he saw was a bedroom wall. Somehow, his room had undergone a remarkable change. Everywhere he looked, he saw greenery. From the ceiling, up the walls, and on his dresser hung ivy, mistletoe, and berries. Each leaf reflected a green tinted light that was almost blinding.

When his eyes adjusted to the brightness, his attention shifted to the bed he had just left. Piled around each side of the bed and the footboard were freshly baked turkeys, hams, and roasts. Mounds of steaming sweet and white potatoes, apples, squashes, pumpkins, and vegetables of every color, size, and shape were heaped in huge bowls. The fresh smell of bread and melted butter filled his nostrils. Candy canes, chocolates, truffles, cookies of all kinds, cakes, nuts, apples, pears, peaches, plums, and foods he couldn't name filled cauldrons in every nook and cranny. The combined aromas of all this bounty made his mouth water.

The food was piled in such a way as to form a throne with a green embroidered chair at the apex. Upon the chair sat a being holding a glowing, yet flameless, light in the shape of a torch. The torch was held high to shed its light on Thomas as he approached. Seeing that he was blinded by the brightness of beacon, the being began to lower the light and said, "Come closer, TJ, and get to know me better."

With the light finally lowered and tilted so as not to obstruct his vision, he was able to see who sat on this throne of plenty.

"Tara," he exclaimed in amazement. "What the hell are you doing up there?"

CHAPTER NINE

"I am the spirit of Christmas present," Tara said with a big smile.

"Are you dead?" Thomas asked in a total state of confusion.

"Um," she said, "I don't think so."

"You're supposed to be over at Uncle— "Thomas suddenly noticed that his sister was transparent. Despite her obvious presence, Thomas was able to see the wall behind her. He squinted and shook his head, but Tara wouldn't take on a solid appearance. "Aren't you over at Uncle Donny's?"

"Well, I thought I was," Tara responded, "but I guess I'm here now. This is so cool." She stood and glided down the pile of plenty.

***

Thomas thought Tara looked beautiful as she descended from her throne. Her golden hair was crowned with a diadem of twelve sparkling silver stars. She wore a gown of emerald trimmed in gold fur. Around her tiny waist was a triple-knotted lavender rope. She was bigger than life and had the air of a queen.

Her smiling face gave Thomas a sense of peace and joy. Torch in hand, she finally stood before him. While small in stature, she was huge in presence.

"You've never seen me like this, have you?"

"Never," Thomas said with a wide grin. "How come I can see through you?"

"Huh?" Tara scanned her own body and saw that Thomas' observation was accurate. "Oh, wow," she exclaimed. "This is really weird." She moved her hand through her midsection. "Jeepers," she said.

With his hand, Thomas did the same and, once again, no substance was there.

Tara began to giggle.

"What's so funny?" Thomas asked. Again, he moved his hand through Tara, only this time at the shoulder.

Tara began to laugh. Her laughter grew and became contagious. Thomas began to chuckle and then he, too, burst into laughter. His eyes began to water, and he held his sides. The two, in the room filled with symbols of plenty, finally gained control of their hysterics and stood in silence.

Wiping the tears from his eyes, Thomas said, "Tara, how did you get here and why are you so ... so see-through?"

Stifling one last giggle, Tara regained her composure and said, "I'm not sure TJ—I mean Thomas. I was asleep at Uncle Donny's and suddenly I heard a voice. It was a man's voice and, for a moment, I was scared. But the voice was very calming and, I don't know, sort of familiar. It said that you needed me and that if I was brave I'd be able to help you. The next thing I knew I was flying, like in Peter Pan. When I looked back at my bed I was still there, but I went through the walls and then, poof, here I am."

"What's with all this food and stuff?" Thomas asked as he waved his hand at the contents of the room.

"Oh, my, I'm only eight and it's hard to remember all

the things the voice said. Wait, I remember!" As if reading from a speech, she said, "It is symbolic of the abundance that exists in the world and that no one really has to go without if we would but share. Is that right?" she asked as if talking to an unseen presence in the air above her. "Yes, Thomas, that's it," she added.

"This is nuts," Thomas said. "Are you really the second spirit I was told to expect?"

"You got it, brother. I am the spirit of Christmas present," she said.

"Okay, little sister. What do we do now?"

"Well, I think you're supposed to touch something. But it isn't me, 'cause your hand goes right through me," she said with a smile. She thought for a moment and once again appeared to be listening to a guiding voice. "Oh, I get it," she said. She held out her torch. "Touch this."

Thomas did as Tara directed and grabbed the torch. The bedroom started to blur. The turkeys, pies, platters, vegetables, strings of holly and berries, and all the other delicious things in the room disappeared. So did the comfort of his bedroom.

They were standing in the middle of a shopping mall. Christmas carols were playing over a PA system. Each store was brightly decorated with snowmen, angels, animated Santas, and blinking lights. Shoppers were loaded with gifts, all wrapped and ready for the tree. The expressions of the shoppers were mixed. Some seemed pleased with their purchases and hummed along with the music. Others looked worried, as if they'd been unable to find the perfect gift. Others were checking lists, and many looked exhausted from their Christmas Eve shopping frenzy. Looking out the mall windows, Thomas saw it was still snowing and he could see the occasional orange blinking lights as plows tried to stay ahead of the storm to clear the access roads and parking spaces.

Tara went to a toy store, Thomas close on her heels. The store was packed, and sales clerks were having a hard time keeping up the customers' demands. Looking through the store window, Thomas saw that every child's dream lay within its four walls. There were cars, trucks, planes, and trains of every make and model. Stuffed bears, dogs, cats, lions, giraffes, and other creatures lined the shelves. Bicycles, tricycles, skateboards, and other wheeled devices were in abundance. Markers, crayons, easels, paints, papers, and other art supplies were plentiful. Board games, electric games, wall games, and an infinite number of other playthings filled the racks. There were big balls, little balls, footballs, soccer balls, baseballs, tennis balls, and every other imaginable ball. There were toys that walked, talked, crawled, and flew. Shelves were filled with construction toys, build-it-yourself toys, and toys that changed from one thing to another. Dolls of all sizes, shapes, and colors, as well as carriages, playhouses, strollers, and play kitchens filled an entire corner of the huge tribute to the desires of children.

Because of the stormy weather, there was bustling activity in the section with wooden sleds, foam sliders, plastic sliders, saucers, and other strange objects meant to race upon the freshly falling snow. Wherever the eye fell, there were dazzling colors and things that whirred, buzzed, bleeped, or clacked. There were toys of war from all the ages and things that represented the stars and the future.

Thomas and Tara entered the wonderland without drawing the least attention. They were wraiths in the world of the present. Occasionally, they would come across husbands and wives quarreling over a choice or the price of an item. Tara would then wave her torch at the couple. Small flecks of light, shimmering like gold dust, would fall on the combatants. Immediately, the arguing stopped and a quick compromise was reached.

"Is there something special about that torch?" Thomas asked.

"I guess there is. It has something to do with spreading light," Tara said.

In the checkout area, Thomas noticed that both customers and clerks were getting frustrated. The occasional credit card that was rejected, a register failing to open, missing UPC codes, checks without addresses, or questionable ID's added tension to the otherwise festive atmosphere. Sensing tempers about to boil, Tara moved to the registers and waved her magic torch. Within moments, the golden dust worked its wonders and scowls turned to smiles. Pushing and shoving transformed into polite excuse me's and you firsts. Spirits lifted and people began to hum along with the carols. Everything seemed to move faster and smoother as courtesy became contagious.

"Tara, aren't these people just wasting their money? Probably half of them can't even pay their bills and these purchases will just drive them further into debt. How many months of paychecks will be wasted buying all this stuff?"

"Oh, my poor Thomas," Tara said. "Don't you think they know that? But, to them, the smiles on their children's faces when they see Santa has come are worth every penny and every sacrifice."

"Santa? There is no Santa. Don't tell me you still believe in Santa Claus?"

In a sweet but sad little voice, she said, "My poor brother. Whatever you believe is real." Her arms opened wide. "None here can see us. Yet I'm real to you, aren't I?" Thomas nodded. "But to them, we don't exist."

Thomas thought for a moment, then said, "But Santa and Christmas is all about getting. It's about greed and big companies ripping everyone off."

"No, Thomas. Christmas and Santa are about giving *and* receiving. People know they're being ripped off. It doesn't matter, Thomas. Every year they choose to be ripped off because they not only make someone else happy, they also make themselves happy. For one brief moment in what is perhaps a life of struggle, they forget their money problems in one little smile or hug or a tear of joy. These things have no price."

"You're a pistol," Thomas said with a grin.

Tara thought for a moment, smiled, and said, "You're right. I am a pistol." She did a little pirouette and glided out of the store.

Thomas followed, but slowed to listen to a couple who obviously hadn't gotten any of the magic gold dust.

"Oh, honey, this is the toy Bradley's been talking about. He says he'll die if he doesn't get one from Santa." The slim woman, somewhere in her early forties, held up a box for her husband's inspection. The tall man with thinning hair took the box from his wife. Thomas could see that the husband was a blue-collar worker with rough hands and years of oil stains embedded in his skin. His clothes were clean, but not new. He turned the box over and looked at the price and his smile quickly faded. He put the box back on the shelf and said to his wife, "I can't afford this."

"Are you sure?" she asked pleadingly.

"You know work is slow this time of year. Our credit cards are maxed, babe. I just don't have the cash. I'm sorry," he said.

"How much do you have in your wallet? Maybe you have enough."

"I only have two twenties," he said. "This is almost ninety bucks."

"Are you sure that's all you have?"

He pulled out his wallet to double check, but he knew he couldn't count what wasn't there.

Thomas thought for a moment. He reached into his pocket for his roll of money. Thanks to his mother and the occasional drug deal, he was usually rolling in dough. *I wonder.* He knew he was not *there*, but maybe some of that dust could help. He looked around, but Tara was nowhere in sight. As the man pulled out his bills, Thomas grabbed a hundred-dollar bill from his own roll. With all the power he could muster in his mind, he took the bill and wished it into the man's hand.

The man counted his bills. "Whoa," he exclaimed. "Where did that come from?" He laid out the bills and there were two twenties *and* a hundred. "Damn," he said to his wife. "That must have been stuck to one of the twenties."

"It's Christmas, you know," his wife said. "Miracles do happen. Does this mean we can ...?"

"You bet we can. Brad will get his heart's desire from Santa this year. Hey, let's check out and then I'll treat you to a burger and fries. After all, it's Christmas." Arm in arm, the happy couple made their way to the checkout counter.

Thomas was grinning from ear to ear. "I don't know how, but I did it," he said. He jumped into the air and kicked his heels together, then pranced out of the store, saying to customers who were unaware of his presence, "I'm a pistol, too."

He looked for his sister. Amid the throng of shoppers, she was hard to spot. Finally, he noticed a section of the mall filled with laughter. Sure enough, Tara was in the middle of the crowd, working her magic. He started toward her, but the ringing of a bell caught his attention. In a corner near a pizza stand was a young girl standing beside a red pot that hung from a tripod. On a small sign near the pot read Salvation Army. The girl ringing the bell was about his age. She was dressed drably, but Thomas thought she was kind of cute. On closer inspection, she looked familiar. "Son of a bitch," he said. "That's Phoebe." Thomas remembered her from a class they had together. He forgot what subject, but he remembered she was the one who always knew the answers to the teacher's questions.

More laughter attracted his attention, not merry this time, but mocking. Near Phoebe and her ringing bell was a group of kids all too familiar to him: Rudy's buddies Josh, Sam, Mike, and Doug. Thomas looked around, but no Rudy. The boys were all in the behavior program at school; they also served as delivery boys for the local drug lord. TJ didn't hang out with them. He didn't hang out with anyone.

Thomas saw the little gang of aspiring hoodlums pointing and laughing at Phoebe. She really is cute, he thought. He decided to go a little closer.

"Hey, Goldilocks, wanna come ring my bell?" Mike yelled. The others laughed.

"Want me to tuck you in tonight? Maybe Santa will bring you a big surprise," Doug said. The little gang burst into laughter.

Thomas could see that Phoebe was shaken. Her nervousness grew when the boys moved toward her. Thomas had a flashback to downtown Hallowell where he'd harassed a woman who was also ringing a bell.

Thomas ran to his sister. He snatched her torch from her small hand and raced back to Phoebe. Tara yelled, "Hey," and dashed after him.

Thomas got to Phoebe just as the boys surrounded her. Raising the torch high, Thomas waved it rapidly, sprinkling the gold dust in all directions and onto each of the troublemakers.

Whatever mischief might have been in the boys' minds quickly vanished.

"Merry Christmas," Sam said.

"Yeah, Merry Christmas," the rest echoed.

Each boy reached into his pocket and emptied cash into the little red kettle.

With a sigh of relief, Phoebe said, "And Merry Christmas to you, Sam, Doug, Josh, and Mike." She looked each boy square in the eye and added, "Thank you."

The boys turned and walked away. They began to

sing "Jingle Bells" and as they walked through the mall, Thomas heard them wishing everyone a Merry Christmas.

Thomas looked at the torch, and then at Tara. He said, "I guess it's still loaded." Tara laughed as she took the magic light from her brother.

He turned to look at Phoebe and then took a step back. Phoebe was looking directly at him. For a moment, her blue eyes that were partly hidden by long blond curls mesmerized him. "Phoebe," he said. She didn't reply.

He turned to Tara, who said, "Phoebe can't see you."

"But ...," he started to say as he looked back to Phoebe. She was looking at him with a questioning expression on her face as though she thought she saw something but couldn't focus on the image. She gave Thomas a cheerful smile and then, with a shrug, returned to her bell ringing.

"I never noticed she was that pretty," Thomas said to Tara.

"That's just one of many things you've failed to notice," Tara replied. "Touch the torch."

Thomas did as she asked, and within seconds, the warmth and joy of the mall dissolved. Thomas found himself out in the furious blizzard looking at a trash barrel fire beneath the Memorial Bridge.

***

"Uh, Tara, why are we here?" Thomas asked in bewilderment. Tara said nothing, but pointed at the fire. Thomas looked more closely. The snow was blinding, and it took his eyes a few moments to adjust to the darkness.

Huddled around the fire were several figures. He was unsure if they were male, female, or a mixture of both. They were heavily bundled in torn and ragged coats. Some had their heads wrapped in rags and others wore what appeared to be camouflage hats. As they held their hands near the fire, he could see that only a few had gloves. The rest had hands either bare or wrapped in cloth. To one side of the fire, he could make out several men chatting as they passed a bottle in a paper bag between them.

"Freakin' bums and winos. They should all just jump off the bridge and save everyone a lot of grief. You know, kill 'em all and let God sort them out," he said and laughed.

Tara wasn't amused. "And who are you to judge who should live or die?" she asked. "I have to wonder if this whole spirit thing is doing you any good, Thomas. You think you know so much, but you're really very stupid sometimes."

"For God's sake, Tara," TJ said, taking the defensive tone he used anytime he was challenged. "These people are worthless. All they do is skulk around garbage cans for food and collect returnable bottles so can they buy booze. They're probably all ex-cons and perverts. One of these days they're going kill someone, then you'll see how right I am."

"Right, Thomas, the headlines are just full of stories of the homeless going on killing sprees. I can't help but wonder which of us is the child. If you're not too scared, let's get closer to this band of perverts and see what's going on." Her words were not a request. Tara turned and walked purposefully over to the abutment, fully expecting Thomas to follow. Grudgingly, he did.

They stopped near the two men passing the bottle of wine. Thomas shot Tara an I-told-you-so look, which she ignored.

"Listen," she said.

"Are going to make it through this one?" the more heavyset of the two men said. He took a swallow of wine, wiped the dribble from his chin with his sleeve, and passed the bottle to the man who looked like he'd be tall if he stood.

"Not sure how many I got left in me," the tall man said. "Each year the dreams get worse, not better. Christmas friggin' Eve and they send us out. The faces of those kids, they seemed so happy to see us. They didn't know Christmas from jack shit. They all came out from their huts when the patrol arrived. Candy, candy, they shouted. They seemed so happy to see us. Jack gave one kid a candy bar, and then the kid gave Jack a grenade in return. He didn't realize what it was until it was too late. Jesus, man, we opened up on that village until there was nothing left standing. Then the V.C. came. It was as if they waited until we wiped out all those villagers before they decided to attack."

"Hey, man, it wasn't your fault," his companion said. "Besides, you got a medal for saving some of your buddies."

"A medal and then a kick in the ass. I just keep seeing those faces smiling and laughing one minute, dead the next. It's worse on Christmas Eve, but every time I see kids I flash back. Can't take it much longer, just can't take it," he said, a tear rolling down his cheek.

"Here, man," the heavy fellow said. "This will help you forget." He passed the bottle to the tall man. The heavy man adjusted his position and Thomas noticed that he had only one leg.

"I see what you mean now, Thomas," Tara said, "definitely worthless. Let's go over by the fire."

As they walked toward the other group, Thomas kept looking back at the two men. The wine must have started to kick in, because he thought he heard laughter. He'd never realized that some of these guys were war heroes who just couldn't deal with the things they'd been required to do. He began to wonder how many hidden secrets and bad dreams were floating around the world. Something to think about, he suggested to himself.

Four other people were huddled around the fire in

the fifty-five-gallon drum: two women, an older man, and a rather young man who was almost a kid. They stood in silence, trying to stay warm. They all wore multiple layers of unmatched clothing in an attempt to stave off the bone-chilling cold.

TJ asked Tara, "So what are their stories?"

"The woman on the left is Mary. Would you believe that she's only thirty-two years old?"

"You're kidding. She looks to be in her fifties maybe," Thomas said in surprise.

"Living on the streets ages a person," Tara replied. "Three years ago she lost her husband and two children when her house burned down."

"No crap," Thomas said.

"No crap, Thomas. She blames herself for the fire. Everything was going great for Mary. She and her husband had good jobs and they lived in a nice house. Her daughter Elizabeth was six and her son Steve was only three. Early one evening, she was ironing some clothes. Her husband and kids had a sudden urge for ice cream and Mary volunteered to go get some. When she got back, the house was in flames. The fire department was there, but there was a kerosene heater near the laundry room and the fire got out of control so fast her husband and kids didn't stand a chance. They told her the cause of the fire was the iron. She apparently forgot to turn it off and left it on her husband's shirt. She's been in and out of treatment, but it's not helping. She knows it was an accident, but she has taken on all of the guilt."

"Man, I'd freak out if that happened to me," Thomas said.

Tara said, "That's exactly what happened to Mary, she freaked out."

Not sure what to say, he asked, "What about that young guy? What's his story?"

"Jimmy? Oh, he's a junkie," Tara said

"So, they don't all have sad stories after all?"

"He was born a junky, Thomas. His parents were heroin addicts and he was born addicted. The parents were dirt poor, so Jimmy never got treatment. When he was sixteen, his parents left the state—welfare fraud—and they left him behind. He's been on the streets for the past five years, alone with no family."

"Jesus, that really sucks," Thomas exclaimed.

"Ya think?"

"What about those two guys?"

Before Tara could answer, they heard a female voice shout, "Okay, you guys, time to go." A woman emerged from the dense snowfall. To Thomas, the voice had a familiar ring. "Come on," the woman said. "I'll not take no for an answer."

Thomas turned to Tara and said, "Lisa? Is that Lisa?

Tara answered, "Yup, that's our mom."

"What the hell is she doing here?" TJ asked, astonished.

"Where the heck have you been? Are you really that

dense? Every Christmas Eve, Mom goes around the city and picks up as many homeless as she can. She takes them to the shelters so they can get a good Christmas meal. And she buys them all a little present. She's been doing that for years."

"Why the hell didn't she say something? You're right, she has disappeared every Christmas Eve since dad died. We'd go to bed and out she went. I thought she was seeing someone or something. Why didn't she say anything?"

"Thomas, she did say something. You just didn't listen. Isn't pot just wonderful? You've been stoned on Christmas Eve for the past three years. Actually, you're stoned almost all of the time. Come on, we have one more stop," Tara said.

"But I want to see what happens," Thomas said.

"Come now," Tara demanded. Thomas gave in and touched the torch.

***

Again, the surroundings melted, then coalesced into Tara's bedroom at Uncle Donny's house. Tara and Billy were still in bed asleep. TJ glanced out the window and saw that the storm had let up and the sun was just beginning to make its Christmas morning appearance.

Spirit Tara looked perplexed. She stared at herself still sleeping in her borrowed bed.

"This is weird," she said. "I'm here, but I'm there." She walked over to herself. "I'm really cute when I'm sleeping." She tried to touch her sleeping self, but her hand passed through her body. "Wow," she said. "This is so cool."

"Is this really Christmas now?"

"Your guess is as good as mine," Tara said. "I'm just along for the ride."

Don, BJ's brother, and his wife Amy live in Manchester. Their home was a nice contemporary on a lake surrounded by mostly wooded land. Don was a logger who, like all loggers, has hit on hard times. His wife is a freelance writer who dabbles in children's books. They had no children. As a result, they'd semi-adopted Tara and Billy and even Lisa. They tried with Thomas, but he rebuffed them.

Thomas started to ask Tara a question but heard Lisa yell from downstairs, "Hey, did you guys forget what day it is?"

The real Tara rolled over, opened her eyes, and bolted out of bed. "Billy, Billy," she shouted, "come on, it's Christmas."

Billy opened his eyes. "Okay, okay." He sat up and stretched his arms in the air. After what seemed like an endless yawn, he asked, "Any word from TJ?"

"I don't think so. I didn't hear him come in last night. Let's go check the other bedroom," Tara said. Some of her enthusiasm for Christmas lessened as she turned to check the other spare room. She was sure her older brother wouldn't be there.

Thomas followed his siblings, knowing the other spare bedroom would be empty. Both Billy and the real Tara saw the empty bed and, in unison, sighed. They sat on the empty bed and neither said a word. Finally, Billy said, "I wish TJ was here." He quickly looked around the room to be sure that his older brother wasn't there to hear his nickname.

"I know," the real Tara said. "Christmas just hasn't been the same since TJ began using … you know … all that drug stuff. Maybe he'll show up, Billy. Just a feeling."

"Doubt it, Sis," Billy said. "I heard Mom telling Uncle Donny she had an argument with him last night."

"Maybe, Billy, but there's something … I don't know … something weird going on. I don't feel like I'm all here," Tara said.

Tara's spirit-self began to laugh. She turned to Thomas and said, "If I only knew I was right here with you. This *is* a bit strange. Thomas, and I think we'll have to go soon. Since she's—I mean I'm awake, I feel like I'm beginning to fade or something."

"Tara, Billy, are you two up?" Lisa yelled from downstairs.

"We're coming, mom," Billy responded.

The spirits of Thomas and Tara began to go downstairs. Thomas observed that Billy and his sister—

the not-spirit one—were moving in slow motion. Thomas looked at Tara, who shrugged her shoulders.

At the bottom of the stairs, Thomas looked into the living room. It was a postcard scene. The Christmas tree, surrounded by beautifully wrapped boxes, stood in front of three large windows overlooking the lake. Everything was covered by freshly fallen snow. Bushes and hedges looked like mounds of snow, and the pines were a beautiful mix of green and white. The sun was rising, and its reddish-gold rays bronzed the sky and reflected in the lake.

"For Christmas morning, you look very sad," Don said to Lisa. Amy was in the shower, so Don thought he'd have a few minutes to chat with his sister-in-law.

"I had hoped so much that he'd show up last night. I wanted to take him with me," Lisa said.

"Did you manage to collect your usual crew?"

"All but one," she told him.

"You know I asked him over. He wanted no part of it. Lisa, you can't let him destroy your life. You have two others who need you," Don said.

"I know, but for some reason, I see Brian when I see TJ. They're so different and yet so much alike. He has his father's spirit, but it's so clouded right now. I can't look him straight in the eye because it makes me so mad that he won't let go and move on. I need him, but he can't see that. So, instead of drawing closer, we push each other away." Tears rolled onto her cheek. "I've lost him, Don,

I've lost him."

Don put his arm around her shoulder in a vain attempt at comfort. "I'll go looking for him later," he said. "Maybe I can get him to come over. In the meantime, you have two kids who truly want to enjoy Christmas. Are you ready for the torture treatment?"

Lisa sniffled and laughed at the same time. "You're right, Don. Let the misery begin." She collected herself just as Billy and Tara came around the corner into the kitchen, their eyes glued to the tree.

"Is breakfast ready, Mom?" Tara asked.

Don and Lisa gave each other a quizzical look. "You mean you want breakfast?" Lisa asked

"Yeah, me too," Billy said.

"Since when? You guys are always in a big hurry to get to the tree," Lisa said.

"We're waiting for something," Tara said matter-of-factly.

"Waiting for what?" asked Lisa

"Don't really know," Tara said. "Breakfast, I guess. I feel really empty."

Not sure how to respond to her children's unusual attitude, Lisa said, "Fine. We have a three-course breakfast that should keep the two of you busy for a real long time."

"Thanks, Mom," Tara said

"Yeah, thanks," Billy added.

Don pulled Lisa aside and asked, "What, has someone

taught them reverse psychology?"

"Beats the hell out of me, but we'll see who can hold out longer," Lisa whispered.

Don grinned and said, "Okay, juice and cereal first.

***

"Thomas, it's time to go," Tara said. "I'm really beginning to fade."

"Can't I stay here? I get the point of all the visits. I screwed up. I realize that now," Thomas said.

"Sorry, big brother, it doesn't work that way. There are still a few things you need to see. You may think you understand, but you'd be surprised how quickly things we think we know fade away. Speaking of fading away, I think I'm going now. Good luck, Thomas, I really hope you make it," Tara said. "We love you."

Tara began to melt away. Her real self, sitting at the breakfast table, seemed dazed. Gradually the spirit of Tara began to flow back into her, and, with a little pop, spirit Tara was gone.

The room began to swirl, making Thomas feel dizzy as everything became a blur. When the spinning stopped, Thomas was back in his room. But it was wrong. It was dark and dank. It smelled of death. The furniture, the walls, and all his possessions were covered in mold, dust, and cobwebs.

CHAPTER TEN

When Thomas sat on the edge of his bed, dust flew into the air. His nostrils filled with the smell of mold and decay. Then, out of the darkness, an apparition formed. The being was tall and cloaked in a flowing black robe; the shape of its head was concealed by the robe's hood. Where there should have been a face, there was nothing but a swirling gray mist. The robe fell to the floor and no feet or footwear were visible.

Thomas had thought that by now he'd be used to strange appearances, but this phantom made his skin crawl and his hands shake.

Even with cotton-mouth, he managed to ask, "Are you the one my father said would come at three?" As soon as the words left his lips, he realized it was a stupid question.

"Are you the spirit of the future?" This, too, was a stupid question, he decided.

Thomas felt like he was about to pee his pants. The *thing* that stood before him was frightening, more because of its ghostly silence than its appearance. It exuded an aura of death and despair that made his heart sink. His mind raced with thoughts of his father's and

Chantelle's deaths. All the mean and senseless things he had done to hurt others roiled to the surface of his consciousness.

Thomas slowly rose from his bed. His shoulders drooped and his knees almost buckled. Only by sheer force of will did he manage to stand straight.

"I don't know if I'll live to see the morning, but I'll go wherever you lead," he said.

The spirit turned the swirling fog of its face toward Thomas, and, for a moment, Thomas thought he'd faint.

"Please speak?"

The spirit didn't. It raised its arm. Although he dreaded the idea, Thomas knew he must touch the being if this night was to end.

The smell of decay quickly gave way to a familiar scent—Hall-Dale High School's cafeteria—and the din of a hundred chatting students. Several teachers mingled with the students, feigning smiles and greetings. It was their daily duty to keep order among the throng of teenagers. Hungry mouths devoured the day's fare, despite its taste or lack thereof.

The spirit stopped and pointed to one of the octagonal blue tables. Thomas moved closer to hear the conversation.

"I don't know any of the details," one of the students said. "All I know is she's dead."

"When did she die?" asked another as he chewed a cold piece of pizza.

"Last night, I guess."

"Any idea how it happened?" one of the girls at the table asked.

"Given all the drugs she took, she probably overdosed. Since she was a kid, they won't give out the details. I'm sure someone will find out and then we'll know for sure," a curly-haired boy replied.

"Hey, maybe we should seek counseling," one of the other girls said. Everyone at the table looked at her and they all burst into laughter.

"Wait, wait," the curly-haired kid said, "what about the funeral?"

"What about it?" a blonde girl asked.

"Hardly anyone will be going. Maybe we should volunteer. We could get out of school."

"Cool idea," chimed in another. "They always serve good food at funerals, too."

"Figures you'd think of the food. Don't you think you should drop a few pounds?"

They all laughed.

"You know, we should go. I was probably her only friend," said a female student with long hair.

"How do you figure that?" the blonde girl asked.

"Well, she always copied my math—when she felt like doing it," he said.

"Yeah, and if you didn't let her she'd kick the crap out of you. For a girl, she was tough."

"Still, she asked me once if I wanted a joint. She said

if I gave her the answers to the test, she'd give me a joint. That was very nice of her."

"You are such a jerk, Austin." The classmate stood and rubbed his knuckles back and forth on Austin's head.

"Quit it," Austin said. The knuckler began to do it again until he noticed the assistant principal had entered the cafeteria and was watching him; he quickly sat down.

Another group of students arrived at the table and the conversation reverted to the usual complaints about homework, tests, and how stupid school was.

Thomas looked at the spirit for some clue as to who had died. The apparition walked away. Its robe brushed against Thomas and he found himself once more in the cold night.

Thomas was in a familiar location, one he had recently visited beneath the Memorial Bridge. This time, though, the scene was different. It was later in the evening. The storm was still raging, but the once robust fire in the barrel was nothing more than glowing embers. It would give little warmth. The men and women who had surrounded the fire weren't visible. Thomas looked around until he spotted several large cardboard crates, the kind that refrigerators come in. They were joined together into a sort of box condo. Thomas saw feet sticking out from the boxes, feet rapidly being covered with snow.

He remembered the two vets drinking under the abutment. They were still there, but showed no signs of life.

"Where's Lisa? Where's my mother?" Thomas asked the spirit. "Lisa is supposed to bring them to the shelter to get warm and get some food," he added.

The spirit gave no response.

Thomas looked in the direction from which his mother had come, thinking that maybe she was just running a little late. He waited and waited, but no one showed.

"My mother has to come," he said. "They'll freeze if she doesn't," he added with panic in his voice.

The spirit pointed towards the two men.

Thomas decided to get a closer look. The tall man, the one with the bad dreams, was barely awake. The heavy man with one leg was passed out, the brown-bagged bottle still clutched in one hand. The blowing snow was beginning to cover his entire body.

Thomas turned to the man who was still awake and screamed, "You've got to find some shelter, all of you. You'll freeze to death if you stay out here."

The man didn't move or respond; he couldn't hear Thomas' plea. Nor would he care, even if he could. There was no one coming this night to shepherd the lost flock to safety. The vet was okay with that. He wanted his nightmares to end, and this night was as good a time as any.

Thomas looked at the spirit for some assurance that either his mother or someone else would bring these people to safety. The spirit pointed at the tall man. Thomas looked and saw that, although the man's eyes were still open, they showed no signs of life. A lone tear was frozen on the man's cheek.

As the silent spirit turned, his black robe once again brushed Thomas' side. The image beneath the bridge swirled into black.

Thomas and the spirit were in the darkened kitchen of his own house.

***

Rather than going to the bridge to gather the homeless, Lisa sat alone in the dark. She had left Don's house with every intention of fulfilling her obligations, but had decided to stop at the house before completing her mission.

When she arrived at the house, TJ was gone. On the kitchen table, she found several roaches in the ashtray and the pungent smell of dope in the air. Lisa was heartbroken. She had hoped that this Christmas would be different.

Lisa grabbed a bottle of Absolut Vodka from the cupboard and poured a double over lots of ice. She hated alcohol straight up. When BJ was alive, they often drank wine or experimented with combinations of liquor and mixes. They never drank much. They only drank socially but never got drunk. BJ said he couldn't stand losing control of his faculties and would never have more than one or two drinks if he had to drive.

Since her husband's death, that had changed. Lisa began making herself vodka martinis, and when she was home, a glass was always in her hand. She followed BJ's rule about drinking and driving, but only if transporting the kids.

She poured herself another double. The lights were still off and she had no intention of turning them on. The only illumination in the house came from the flickering reds, blues, and greens on the Christmas tree. She picked up one of the roaches and took a sniff. She twirled it between her fingers until the white paper disintegrated and the pot began to stain her fingers. She watched as the last of the crushed weed dropped and scattered onto the breakfast counter, not caring that it missed the ashtray.

Lisa was tired, tired from the alcohol, tired from her arguments with Thomas, tired from loneliness, tired from failure, and tired of life.

No time to be tired, she thought, pouring another double and taking a big swallow. Her mouth and throat were so numb she hardly noticed the burning sensation as the liquid seeped into her bloodstream.

"You've got to stop her," Thomas shouted at the uncaring spirit. "Make her stop drinking. Please."

The black-robed arm lifted and pointed toward his mother.

Thomas looked and saw her stagger as she got up off the stool. "Where the frig are they?" she said aloud. "Oh, they are rrright heah." Lisa began to laugh. She picked up her keys, dropped them, and picked them up again. Her head spun, and she almost fell to the floor. "Heah," she said again and broke out in hysterics.

"Mom, listen to me. I'm right here. I'm going over to Uncle Donny's. I'll be there for Christmas. Mom, you can't drive," Thomas shouted.

"Tis the season to be jolly, fa, la, la, la … la, oh, frig it," she said. She took a last swallow of vodka and went to the door. Her hands fumbled at the handle in the darkened kitchen.

"Mom! You can't drive like this. You're drunk. Please, I love you, don't do this," Thomas pleaded, tears streaming from his eyes.

For a moment, Lisa stopped and turned in his direction.

Hoping that somehow she heard him, Thomas said, "Mom, I love you. You have to stay here. You can't drive."

Lisa shook her head and, finding the door handle, went out into the blizzard. She left the door open, letting the snow blow into the kitchen.

Thomas looked at the spirit and pleaded, "Make her stop. Please, make her stop." Getting no response,

Thomas turned and started for the door. Before he took more than three steps, the room began to melt. He knew what was happening and screamed, "Nooooooooooo."

***

Thomas was not at home. He wasn't sure where he was. It was a party, but Thomas didn't recognize anyone. The lights were low, and the music was blaring. He could smell the beer and the all too familiar aroma of burning marijuana. As he looked around, he saw some of the kids were popping pills. Some were lighting bowls. Others were snorting. *My God, this is a regular drug store.* Several couples were dancing, or, rather, groping. Young girls in short skirts and tops that barely covered their breasts were moving their hips ways that were very inviting to their male—and sometimes female—partners. Some boys let their hands slide along the thighs and bare waists of the obviously uninhibited girls. Thomas was aroused by the sensuous moves. And, although he couldn't be seen, he moved among the couples and pretended to partake in the dance.

Remembering his mother, he quickly moved to stand beside his ghostly guide and began to view the party with new eyes. This was his life, suspected but not seen by his mother. *Sex, drugs, and rock 'n' roll. Get what you can and care for no one, because no one cares for you.*

It looked different to him now. *These kids are going*

nowhere. Tomorrow their heads will burst, their guts will ache, and they won't have any idea what they did tonight. He knew some of the guys would "get lucky" with the girls they'd plied with drinks, hits, and snuffs. Girls who would remember little. A few would get pregnant and be unable to name their babies' fathers. This far gone, safe sex was not a priority.

When Thomas had been at these parties, it all seemed cool. Now it all looked dumb.

There *were* people who cared. People who went out in the middle of a storm to bring those in need to someplace warm, someplace with a little food, someplace that gave a reassuring touch. Those same people had wants, needs, hopes, and desires. They also had their share of problems, disappointments, and broken hearts.

"I've been so selfish, so caught up in my own little world at the expense of others," Thomas whispered.

A movement caught his attention. A boy and a girl were swaying their way up the stairs. The girl was so out of it, she could barely stand. The boy was taking pleasure in steadying the girl by holding her bottom. The girl missed a step and almost fell back down the steps. She began to giggle at her own ineptness. It was a giggle that sounded familiar, older, but definitely familiar. The boy helped her up. As she regained her footing, she turned and looked directly at Thomas. Tara. Not his younger sister of Christmas present, but an older version, maybe fifteen or sixteen. She continued to look at him, almost as if she could actually see him. Then the boy grabbed her hand and began to yank her up the stairs.

Thomas started to rush towards his baby sister. She turned to look at him once more, seeming confused and disoriented.

Thomas yelled, "Tara." She looked at him again as if pleading—pleading that what she was seeing was true. Thomas literally ran *through* the bodies of those present. He reached the stairs and began his ascent to rescue his sister. She held out a hand, hoping to touch the flesh of what she knew had to be a dream. Just as Thomas was about to grab her, a loud, shrill sound forced him to stop. He turned and saw that the spirit had its head thrown back, resembling a wolf in mid-howl.

Tara was gone. The entire room was gone.

Thomas stood at the center of blackness.

***

A single light hung from the ceiling. It had no shade, just a bulb at the end of a very short chord. Thomas was dizzy. Time was skipping in leaps and bounds. He lost track of the date, even the year. Thomas didn't know if the events he was being shown were certainty or possibility.

Thomas was standing outside a jail cell. As his eyes

grew accustomed to the dim light, he realized it wasn't a jail, but a prison. In its usual fashion, the spirit pointed to one of the barred cells. Thomas saw two boys. They were maybe fifteen or sixteen. It was hard for him to tell; their hair was cut short, and the bright orange uniforms were too baggy to give him any true indication of their size.

"What are you in for?" The shorter of the two asked the other.

"Got caught dealing crack," came the answer. His voice sounded familiar. "You?"

"Same shit, selling drugs. I think half the kids in here are drug pushers. You look familiar. Is your name Thomas?"

The taller boy laughed. "No, you've got me confused with my brother. My name is Billy. Billy Johnson."

"Yeah, yeah, that's right. I heard that he had a kid brother working the streets. Where is Tommy-boy these days?"

"Prison."

"What they bust him on?"

"He's in for murder," Billy said.

"Shit, man, is he going to get the needle or something?"

"Life."

"Why did old Tommy-boy waste someone?"

"When my mother died in a drunken accident on Christmas Eve, he flipped," Billy said, a shadow of pain crossing his face.

"Christmas Eve? Man, that really sucks."

"That's not the half of it. My father was killed in Iraq on Christmas."

"Holy crap, dude! What are the chances of that? No wonder he flipped."

"Yeah, after that, he got deeper into drugs and pulled some small jobs for money. Then he turned mean. There was no talking to him. We moved to our uncle's, but even he couldn't help. Thomas was just too far gone, wouldn't listen to anyone about anything."

"Can't blame him, dude. That would have sent me over the edge, too. So, did he kill someone in a robbery or a drug deal or something?"

"No, he killed the guy that got my sister hooked on crack. She was at a party …"

***

Once again, the spirit of Christmas future hurled Thomas through time. He couldn't believe his little brother was in jail. He couldn't believe that in a time yet to come he could kill someone.

There appeared to be no true order to his time travel. He had hoped to hear his brother's story, but the spirit seemed intent on showing only incomplete futures, as if they were — perhaps — not cast in stone.

Thomas was now standing before a tall wrought-iron

gate on State Street. The sky was dark and pouring rain. Lightning blazed above, and booming thunder hurt his ears. This experience was real. In all his other travels, he'd been immune to the elements and was neither bothered nor touched by wind or snow. He grew frightened by this reality.

Once more, the finger pointed to his destination.

"But why here, Spirit?"

Again, the spirit didn't respond, but merely kept its finger out. Slowly, the iron gates opened, and Thomas was guided, almost by force, to walk in a particular direction. He wound up in a remote corner of the cemetery. He was wet and cold. He stood before a grave overgrown with weed and grass.

"Before I look," Thomas said, his hands shaking from cold and fear, "let me ask you one question. Are the things you've shown me things that are going to happen? Isn't there any way of changing the future?"

The spirit pointed at the grave, ignoring his question.

"Spirit," Thomas demanded. Water coursed down his face, his matted hair offering no protection. "I know I'm not very smart. The things I've been shown make me look pretty stupid. But I do know that if a person follows a certain path, he'll go where that path takes him. Is it possible to change our destination by taking another path? Can't we take a right turn and go somewhere else? Is what you have shown me what *will* happen, or what *might* happen?"

The spirit pointed to the grave.

Thomas looked at the marker and read the name.

"Oh, God! Not Tara, not my sister. That should be me, not my baby sister."

Thomas fell to his knees. "Please, Spirit, don't let this happen. I've changed. I know I've screwed up. Do you show me this just to torture me or is there still hope?"

The spirit's hand began to shake.

Thomas pleaded, "Spirit, I *have* changed. I was blinded by my own selfishness and self-pity. Please, help me. Don't let these things happen. I understand what I've been shown. I understand. I see things I didn't want to deal with before. I know my mother, Tara, and Billy love me. I know if I keep screwing up I'll totally mess them up. I don't want that to happen. I … I … love them too much. I don't want to hurt them. Tell me I can change things."

Thomas reached out and grabbed the spirit's hand. It tried to pull back, but Thomas held fast. "Please," Thomas prayed aloud. "Please."

The spirit began to shake even more and started to transform. For a moment, Thomas thought he was being taken to another time. Suddenly, the spirit vanished. Instead of its hand, Thomas found himself clutching his own pillow. He was back in his own room.

CHAPTER ELEVEN

 Thomas peered anxiously around his room. Everything was in its proper place. His hands held his pillow, not the cold limb of an otherworldly being. He squeezed the pillow and tossed it in the air several times. He laughed and kept throwing the pillow in the air as he shouted, "It's my pillow. Just a pillow. *My* pillow."

After several moments, he stopped and hugged it to his chest. As he caught his breath and sat back against the headboard, he once again looked around the room, half expecting to see another apparition. All was quiet and normal. He glanced at his clock radio. The digital display read 7:00 a.m.

He suddenly heard dull laughter coming from outside his window. What day was it?

"Crap. What day is it?" he asked aloud. Thomas scrambled off the bed and rushed to the window. Still hearing voices, he grappled with the lock and flung open the sash. A rush of cold air filled his lungs and the morning sun reflecting off the snow made him squint until his vision adjusted to the brightness. Scanning the scene below, he whispered aloud, "Holy crap."

The universe was blanketed in snow at least three feet

deep. Everything was white—rooftops, trees, shrubs, roads, even the Kennebec River was a blaze of pure white haunted by only a hint of color as the rising sun's light refracted in the frozen water crystals.

Again, laughter caught his attention. Two boys were trudging through the waist-high snow. They fell, laughed, and fell again, almost disappearing with each slip of the foot.

"Hey," Thomas shouted. "Hey, you guys."

The two boys searched for the origin of the voice. They were almost across from Thomas' house, and, as Thomas waved his arms, the movement caught the boys' attention. They turned and looked up. One pointed his finger at himself, "You mean us?"

"Yes, you," Thomas yelled back. "What day is this?"

They looked at each other quizzically. One shouted, "What do you mean?"

"I mean, what day is this? Don't you understand English?"

"We understand English," one replied.

"Are you high or something?" the other asked.

"No, no," Thomas said. "I've been sick and lost track of the days."

The kids exchanged knowing looks. They were brothers who lived a few houses down and had seen Thomas several times when he was high.

Thomas hollered, "Seriously guys, what day is it?"

"It's Christmas," they shouted and broke into

laughter.

As they continued through the snowdrifts Thomas said, "Merry Christmas." The brothers waved and continued on their journey.

"Yes," Thomas shouted. "Christmas. It's Christmas."

Thomas ran to his sister's bedroom, only realizing when he reached her door that no one was home. He bolted back to his room.

"Crap, they're over at Uncle Donny's. Wait, that's good. It means everything is as it should be. Everything's the same. Except me," he proclaimed.

A sudden scraping noise made him cringe. He looked around the room hoping not to see another spirit. The noise grew louder.

"Snowplow. The plows are out. Great, I thought I'd be stranded here all day," Thomas said as he headed for his closet in search of a winter jacket. He opened the closet and grabbed his navy-blue pea coat. He felt the bulge in the inner pocket. He pulled out a bag of weed, studied it, sniffed it, and said, 'This will come in handy later," and stuffed it back in the pocket.

He went to his dresser, opened the bottom drawer, pulled out a stash of rolled bills and stuffed them into his jeans. Darting for the door, he came to a quick stop. Turning slowly, he surveyed the room that, only a few moments earlier, had been the scene of mind-blowing experiences, better than the best of highs.

"Thanks, Dad," Thomas said to nowhere in particular.

"Thank you so very much."

Spinning on the balls of his feet, he charged out of the room, down the stairs, and out the kitchen door. Despite the cold, the lack of wind and the bright sun made it seem like a cold spring day. Thomas had to trudge through the waist-high snow in the driveway. but, once he broke through to the road, it was relatively snow-free. Again, Thomas came to a halt, took a deep breath. and looked at the fairy-tale scene. Snow-covered rooftops whose chimneys exhaled slowly rising columns of smoke added to the charm of the village. The smell of burning wood gave him a sense of comfort and warmth.

"Okay, what am I doing?" he said. He thought for a moment. "Presents, got to find some presents." With a sense of purpose, he began to head downtown.

The road was slippery. It would take several passes of the plow to even come close to seeing pavement. As he slipped and slid down the street, Thomas began to laugh. He thought anyone watching him would be amused, betting how long he'd stay on his feet. A car crawled by and Thomas waved and yelled, "Merry Christmas." The car honked back.

Sliding around the corner by Hatte's Restaurant, he stopped once more. He looked right and then left. There were no cars parked at the shops.

It's Christmas, you jerk. No one will be open.

Then it hit him, the tantalizing aroma of baking bread tinged with a slight hint of cinnamon.

"The bakery's open," he said and started down the street, his nose leading the way. When he got to Slate's the sign in the window said: Open Christmas Morning Until 10:00 a.m. No cars were out front, but several patrons were in the shop, probably folks who lived in walking distance. As Thomas opened the door, a set of bells tied with green and red ribbons announced his entrance. Two older men, a woman, and the baker turned to see who came in. Thomas didn't know them, but they knew him.

The baker said, "Look, son, we don't want you messing with our Christmas, so please go someplace else."

At first surprised by the rebuke, Thomas recalled the numerous times he'd gone in there while he was stoned and given those present a hard time.

"I'm sorry, sir," Thomas replied. "Merry Christmas and I promise I'll never be rude to you or anyone else ever again. Those days are gone."

Thomas then looked at the other customers and said, "And Merry Christmas to you, too." The customers gingerly returned the sentiment.

"We'll see," the baker said. "Since it's Christmas, I suppose I can give you a break. But I warn you …."

"Trust me, I've turned a new leaf. No more problems, ever," Thomas said.

"Okay, boy, like I said, it's Christmas. What can I do for you?"

Thomas said, "Thank you sir," and looked at the display cases. "Tell you what, get four of your biggest boxes and load them up with a little of everything, the sweeter and prettier the better."

The baker gave him a look Thomas understood. He reached into his pocket and pulled out the roll of bills. The baker smiled and said, "Coming right up, young man."

The boxes were stuffed full of cookies, rolls, decorated breads, cinnamon sticks, twirls, and all kinds of frosted things, then put them into two large shopping bags. Thomas paid the bill, grabbed the bag handles, and wished them all a Merry Christmas once more. The other patrons began to chat and paid no more attention to Thomas, who was trying to figure out how to open the door without putting the bags on the slushy entrance floor. He finally managed to turn the handle and used his rear to push the door open and he backed out. Finally outside, he turned quickly and ran right into two girls who were also going to the bakery.

Thomas was standing nose to nose with Phoebe, the girl from the mall, and her red-haired friend, Stella. For a moment, Thomas and Phoebe just stared at each other. Realizing how close they were, Phoebe took a step back; Thomas had no room to retreat since his back was almost against the door.

Thomas smiled and said, "Hi."

Phoebe was wearing a fuzzy purple beret and

matching scarf and mittens. Her cheeks were rosy from the cold and her eyes sparkled. She smiled back and said with a giggle, "Hello."

Not wanting to be left out, her friend Stella said, "Hi."

Just noticing the friend, Thomas said, "Oh, hi, and Merry Christmas to both of you."

The girls both smiled, although Thomas only saw Phoebe's.

"Your name is Phoebe, right?" he asked.

Amazed that he knew her name, she lowered her eyes a little and said, "Yes, and your name is Thomas."

Encouraged by her knowledge, Thomas said, "Yup, but my friends call me TJ. You can call me TJ."

Phoebe wasn't accustomed to attention from boys. She was thought of as cute, but something of a wallflower. Both girls went a little big-eyed and averted their gazes from both each other and TJ.

"Hey, Phoebe," TJ said, "would you mind if I gave you a call sometime? You know, to talk about school and stuff."

Phoebe grabbed Stella's hand. Her cheeks got even rosier and her mouth went dry. None of the boys in her class gave her the time of day unless they needed help with their homework. Taking a deep breath, she said, "That would be nice, TJ. Really nice."

Feeling a wave of confidence, TJ said he'd call her right after Christmas and that maybe they could hang out over the break. He apologized that he had to get going but promised that he'd definitely be in touch.

As the girls opened the bakery door, the three other people in the shop came out; they let the older folk pass and wished them a happy holiday.

Just as the door was about to close, Phoebe said to TJ, "Were you at the … oh, never mind. Don't forget to call."

"Oh, I won't," TJ said with a wink.

***

TJ and Phoebe exchanged a brief smile through the window. Then an idea hit him. He went a couple of shops down and looked in the window of the one named LUX. The carousel was still there. His mother had always wanted it but wouldn't buy it for herself. He searched through the glass for any sign of movement in the shop, but he saw no one. All the lights were off.

"Damn," he muttered. He tried knocking on the door. Nothing happened. Saddened, he began to leave, but when he reached the corner of the building, he noticed a set of outside steps to the second floor. Encouraged, he put his bags on the lower snow-covered step and went up the stairs. As he went, he kicked the snow off with a sliding motion of his feet. When he reached the small landing at the top he saw a light on inside and heard a radio playing Christmas music.

Looking through the glass-paned door, TJ saw a white-haired man with glasses sitting at a small, round

breakfast table. In one hand was a cup and in the other hand was a pencil. There was a newspaper spread out on the table. Not wanting to startle the old man, TJ gently knocked on the door. Getting no response, TJ knocked a little harder. The man jerked his head up and looked to the door. TJ smiled at the old man who slowly rose from the chair after taking a sip from his cup. The old man opened the door.

"What can I do for you, son?"

"Merry Christmas," TJ replied.

"Same to you, son. Come in, come in, I don't need to heat all of Hallowell. Cost of fuel is bad enough. Ayuh, they get you coming and going, they do."

"Thank you, sir," TJ said. "I only need a moment of your time. Tea."

"What, you want some tea?" the old man asked.

"Oh, no, I mean you're drinking tea," TJ said.

Not sure where the conversation was going or if the boy was in his right mind, the old man asked, "Did you come to see if I was drinking tea?"

"No, I'm sorry. I came to see if you could sell me something from the shop."

"You do know it's Christmas, right? Guess you must since you wished me Merry Christmas. We're closed on holidays, boy."

"I know, sir, and I'm really sorry to be bothering you. But I've been real sick lately and I couldn't get out shopping. My mother really wants something from your store and this is the first chance that I've been able to get out and get her a present."

The old man gave TJ a solid once-over and said, "Aren't you the older Johnson boy? Your dad was killed a few years back in Iraq?"

"Yes, sir. My name is TJ."

"Hmm, yes, I've heard the name before. Not a very popular young man, are you? Leastwise, not with some of the local merchants."

"You're right, sir. But you see, that's what I meant by being sick. I'm better now and I really need to get my mother that present." TJ's eyes began to water, which didn't go unnoticed by the old man.

"Well, that may be true, may not be true. At least you're thinking about your mother and not yourself."

TJ was amazed that he was so widely known by the townsfolk—and not in a positive way.

"What item are we talking about, anyway?"

Encouraged, TJ said, "The carousel in the window."

"Ayuh, thought so," the old man said. "Your mother's had her eye on that for some time now. She comes in every now and again and ask to wind it up. Course, I always say okay. Hard to refuse that pretty smile. Could have sold that ole carousel a dozen times, but I keep the price too high. Guess I was waiting for the right customer. Suppose that could be you. Follow me, son."

The old man went to a door off the kitchen that led them directly to the shop below. He said, "Watch your head now. I've got stuff hanging everywhere. My missus used to take care of the clutter, but when she passed on my heart just went out of being neat and tidy, I guess."

TJ followed the man through the crowded antiques. The place was so packed he had to keep twisting and turning to avoid knocking items over. The old man moved easily. He probably could've done it in his sleep, TJ figured. After years of dealing with customers in the crowded shop, his steps were second nature.

The man cleared a spot off an old writing table. He grabbed the carousel and set it in the cleared space. TJ moved to get a closer look. The piece was immaculate. The colors were as brilliant as they'd been the day it was made and the detail on the horses amazed him. The old man watched as TJ marveled at the treasure from times gone by.

Spotting the key on the side, TJ gave the old man a look as if to ask permission to turn it.

"Go ahead, crank her up."

Not wanting to break the spring, TJ cautiously turned the key. When he stopped, the carousel came to life. As it turned, the painted horses, sliding up and down on the brass poles, seemed to him to be enjoying their rebirth. TJ didn't know the music. It was carnival music.

Then TJ saw the price tag by the key. $500. No wonder it hadn't sold.

The old man chuckled as he saw TJ's expression as he spotted the price. He said, "Well since it's for your mother and it's Christmas Day, you can have it for two-fifty."

TJ reached into his pocket and pulled out the roll of bills. He counted his money, but it totaled only a hundred and forty-five dollars. TJ's shoulders dropped in disappointment.

"Here's the deal," the old man said. "I'll take a hundred now and the rest you can work off. No more cash, just work. For the next six months, you'll come here Saturday mornings and clean the shop. That includes dusting and polishing all these fine items."

The old man knew what he offered was not a glamor deal for a young man, but he wanted to see how much "better" TJ really was.

"You mean it?" Thomas asked. "That'd be great. You tell me the time and I'll be here. There won't be a lick of dust on a thing. Thank, you, thank you so much, Mister … I'm sorry, I don't know your name."

"Call me Mr. Parrish. I'm glad you're so enthused now. We'll see how you feel after you do all this glassware and porcelain. Okay, it's a deal and you can start on Monday, since you're on vacation. Seven a.m., and I don't like to be kept waiting."

"No, sir—I mean, yes, sir, Mr. Parrish. Monday at seven sharp. Merry Christmas, sir."

The shopkeeper went to a back room and emerged with a box covered in holiday décor. The box was perfect for the carousel, as if intended for that very purpose.

"Mr. Parrish, do you know if I can get a taxi today? I must get out to Manchester. My whole family's out there."

"I know a guy who'll take you there. I'll give him a call. And you probably ought to get those pastries you left outside. It's nice out, but they might freeze. Use the front door, but be sure to lock it back up when you come in." He went to the back of the shop and began dialing the phone.

"How did you know about the—"

The old man waved his hand in the air.

After about a fifteen-minute wait, a taxi pulled up front. TJ thanked his benefactor profusely and promised again that he wouldn't let him down, that he'd be back Monday.

TJ loaded his presents into the taxi and they made their slow way to Augusta and out Western Avenue to Manchester.

CHAPTER TWELVE

The trip to TJ's uncle's house took twice as long as normal. There was little traffic, but the road conditions were rugged. Driving was slow and slippery as the bright sun turned snow to icy slush. When they reached the house, TJ was certain he'd missed Christmas gift-giving. He asked the driver how much for the ride but was told that the trip was a present, that the old man said him to save his money for his new girlfriend. TJ shook his head in astonishment and muttered, "How does he do that?"

Juggling his three packages, TJ plowed his way through the four hundred feet of the deep snow in the driveway that had yet to be cleared. Finally, puffing from his trek, he reached the front door. The house was so far back from the main road that no one had heard the taxi drop him off. Setting his packages on the covered porch, TJ knocked on the door. He waited for what seemed an eternity, but, at last, he heard the door handle turn and Lisa opened the door.

She looked tired. Too little sleep and too much tension were taking a toll. The only barrier between them was a glass-paned storm door.

"Hi, Mom. Merry Christmas," TJ said.

"What did you say?" Lisa asked as she opened the glass door.

Perplexed, TJ repeated, "Hi, Mom, Merry Christmas."

"Yeah, I heard the Merry Christmas part. But please repeat the *hi* part," Lisa said.

Now understanding what she meant TJ said, "Hi, Mom."

"Oh, my God, Thomas, you said 'hi, Mom.' Do you know how long it's been since you called me Mom?"

"Not sure exactly, but way too long, I guess." Tears ran down his face. He held out his arms and Lisa grabbed her son and practically squeezed all the air out of his lungs. He gladly endured the pain. He hugged back with all the strength that he could muster.

After a few moments, TJ said, "Can I come in?"

"Oh, my God, yes."

He started to go in, but remembered the packages. He collected them and crossed the threshold. Tara came tearing around the corner from the living room. She looked up at TJ and said, "It's about time. Where have you been? We haven't opened a single present because I was waiting for you. I told everyone you'd be here, but no one believed me. And … what's that French word? Oh, yes, voilà, here you are. A little earlier would have been nice, you know. I'm stuffed and can't eat another thing. I think I'm going to bust."

TJ reached down and scooped his little sister into a hug. His tears began to flow once again.

Tara said, "You know, big brother, I had the strangest dreams last night. I bet you did, too." She spoke with little sobs between her words.

"Yeah, little sister, I had some pretty strange dreams. It just so happens that you were the big star of one of them."

TJ set her down but held on to her hand.

"Well, of course, I was a star, I was born to greatness." She started to giggle, and soon they both succumbed to laughter.

Lisa looked at them as if they'd lost their minds. Hearing all the laughter, Billy came sliding around the corner. The hardwood floors were like ice for stockinged feet. Upon seeing his brother, Billy grinned from ear to ear.

"Hi, TJ," Billy shouted. "Oops." Saying TJ instead of Thomas always brought a stinging punch to the arm.

TJ stopped laughing and moved towards Billy. His face was serious, and his brother braced for the worst. TJ said, "Merry Christmas, Billy," and gave him a big hug.

"Are you okay?" asked Billy as the big squeeze subsided.

"I'm perfect, Billy. In fact, I want you to hit me in the arm as hard as you can. From now on, call me TJ. You owe me lots of hits, so give me one now. You deserve your revenge," TJ said in a monster-like tone.

Billy thought for a moment and said, "Nah, it's okay. It's Christmas. I don't want to hit you."

"Okay," TJ said. "But from now on it's TJ. And anytime you want to take a poke, you go right ahead. I swear I will never hit you again, unless—"

"Unless what?"

"You'll understand in a minute."

Lisa was in a state of shock. She couldn't believe the transformation in TJ. She kept looking at his eyes to see if they were dilated or any other telltale sign of being high. If he *was* stoned, she couldn't see it.

Sensing his mother's scrutiny, he turned to her and smiled.

"Mom, I am not on anything and I never will be again. I promise. So, I see you haven't done the tree yet." He peered around the corner into the living room.

Tara said, "No, we haven't. We've been waiting for guess who?"

Even though everyone had been up early, they'd all taken their time eating and just mop around. Without saying so, they expected something, but no one dared to say exactly what. Tara kept smirking at the breakfast table as if she knew something the rest didn't, but, when asked, she ignored the questioning and changed the subject.

"Where are Uncle Donny and Aunt Amy?" TJ asked.

"Look out the back window," Lisa said.

Off in the distance, he could barely make out two figures on cross-country skis. "Figures," TJ said. "They love all that outdoors stuff."

"After a long—and very large—breakfast, they decided to work off a few calories. It's so pretty out. I can't blame them for wanting to take in such a gorgeous morning," Lisa said.

TJ took off his jacket and hung it on the coat tree by the door. He then picked up the bags, walked into the living room, and beheld spectacle of the tree with its mountain of presents.

"So," Tara said, "what's in the bags?"

"Given how much you guys ate, probably nothing you really want at this point," TJ replied.

Tara pulled a pastry box out of one of the bags and looked inside. Her eyes lit up at all the goodies, but her rebellious tummy gurgled at the thought of consuming more food. "They look scrumptious," Tara said, "but I'm afraid I'll have to wait a little while before I even think about eating anything else. We all appreciate the thought, dear brother." She grabbed his hand and pulled him down for a kiss.

"What's in that bag?" Billy asked. "It's not from the bakery."

"I'll show you in a minute, but first something else," TJ said. He walked back to his jacket and reached into his inner pocket. He pulled out the bag of dope and brought it over to Billy. Lisa gasped.

"Billy, see this?" TJ said. "This is the *unless*. If I ever, ever see you around any of this stuff, you and I are going to have a private talk. Get my drift, little brother?"

Seeing the absolute sincerity in TJ's eyes, Billy gulped and said, "Yes, sir!"

Lisa was finally able to take a breath. TJ turned to his mother and said, "Please follow me." He walked to the bathroom, opened the toilet, dumped the contents of the bag, and proudly sent the weed into the land of two thousand flushes.

Lisa gave TJ a happy smile and once again gave him a hug. "Thank you, thank you."

Both Tara and Billy cheered and joined in for a group hug.

TJ led them all back into the living room and grabbed the bag from LUX. He removed the box from the bag and turned to Lisa.

"Merry Christmas, Mom. I love you," he said.

"Just hearing those words is the best present I could ever receive, TJ," Lisa said as tears of pure joy streamed down her cheeks.

Lisa set the box on a table and removed the cover. "Oh, my God, TJ, where did you ever find this? Old Man Parrish sold the carousel he had two years ago, and I thought I'd never see one like it again."

"What?" TJ said. "I bought this from Mr. Parrish this morning."

"That's impossible, TJ. Mr. Parrish died last year. He was very old, you know, and I hear he went peacefully at his own kitchen table. They say he was drinking a cup of tea and—"

"Doing a crossword puzzle?"

"Yes, that's right," Lisa said. "But how did you know that?"

"Mom, you wouldn't believe it if I was capable of telling you," TJ said, shaking his head in astonishment.

"I would," Tara interjected.

"Yes, you would, Tara," TJ said. "I just bet you would."

"Well, his son must have found another one. He took over the store after his father died. Odd that he could find one exactly the same as the other. Thank you so much, my dear. I will cherish this always."

"Okay, gang, there are two other people in this room who have been chomping at the bit to open those pretty presents under that beautiful tree," Tara said.

Lisa and TJ burst into laughter.

"Let's do it," Lisa said.

"This is the best Christmas ever," Tara said.

"It certainly is," Lisa said, with a tiny hint of sadness in her voice.

TJ gave her a hug, and they watched as Tara and Billy tore into the sea of gifts.

"He's with us, you know, Mom. I mean he is *really* with us," TJ said. He missed his dad, but he also felt a great deal of inner comfort knowing that his father was done and could now move on.

"I know he is, TJ," Lisa said. "I feel him now and I felt him really strong last night. He was watching over me during the storm as I was collecting my strays."

"Is the man who has the bad dreams okay?"

"How do you know about him?"

"Oh, I have my sources," TJ said.

"You and I are going to have a sit-down. Some strange things have been going on, and I think you know more than you're letting on," Lisa said as she poked him in the rib.

"TJ, come look at this stuff," Billy yelled. "Way cool. Merry Christmas, you guys. This is great."

Tara turned to TJ and Lisa and said, "Yeah, Merry Christmas." She winked at TJ as they both came over to celebrate the joys of giving and receiving.

About the Author

Mr. Harris was born in Massachusetts and currently resides in Maine. He received his degree in Political Science from The American University in Washington, D.C. and completed graduate work in Public Administration, Planning & Community Development. He has worked at almost every level of government

He is co-author of the controversial novel *Waking God: The Trilogy*, coined a "spiritual thriller." He wrote *Jesus Taught It, Too: The Early Roots of the Law of Attraction*, and other titles that can be found on his author page on Amazon.com.

ALL THINGS THAT MATTER PRESS

FOR MORE INFORMATION ON TITLES AVAILABLE
FROM
ALL THINGS THAT MATTER PRESS, GO TO
http://allthingsthatmatterpress.com
or contact us at
allthingsthatmatterpress@gmail.com

**If you enjoyed this book, please post a review on
Amazon.com and your favorite social media sites.
Thank you!**

www.ingramcontent.com/pod-product-compliance
Lightning Source LLC
Chambersburg PA
CBHW060426260626
47161CB00005B/1798